A LOVE SO DANGEROUS

TO THE BONE BOOK ONE

LILI VALENTE

A LOVE SO DANGEROUS

To The Bone
Book One

By Lili Valente

❀ Created with Vellum

ABOUT THE BOOK

GABE: I have zero interest in Happily Ever After. I just want to feel alive, to look into a woman's eyes and see something that's going to keep my mind off all the shit I refuse to think about for an hour or two.

And then I meet her, a good girl with a body made for sin and ugly problems only a bad man can fix.

A bad man like me…

CAITLIN: Gabe Alexander is the devil. Or an angel.

He's a criminal hiding behind a million dollar pedigree, but he also saved my life and my family. He's the worst kind of bad news, but every time he touches me, and whispers filthy, beautiful things in my ear, all I want is more.

More of his kiss, his touch, and the dangerous, seductive things he makes me feel.

I don't want to go bad, but the man makes it feel so damned good...

Warning: A Love So Dangerous is the first in a three part series. It is a full-length novel that ends in a cliffhanger.

"And softness came from the starlight
and filled me full to the bone."

— W.B. YEATS

CHAPTER 1

CAITLIN

"Forgetting a debt doesn't mean it's been paid" –Irish
proverb

*I*n a week, it will all be over.

In a week, the pieces of my family
will be scattered like dandelion seeds in a hard wind
and there's not a thing I can do about it.

Deep down, I know that. I know this time the
Cooneys are so screwed there will be no sweet-
talking our way out of trouble. Still, I keep shifting
the bills around on the scarred kitchen counter and
punching numbers into my calculator, hoping to
find a way to keep the balls in the air and the kids
out of the system.

But the state doesn't care that I've been running
this family since I was seventeen and doing a pretty
good job of it until now. My father's the legal

guardian. All it will take is a hard look in our direction—the kind of hard look that will come when we get kicked out of the house and the kids start going to school smelling like they're living in a van—and it will become obvious that Chuck is an unfit parent. Before you can say "throw the baby out with the bathwater," the four underage Cooneys will be scooped up by the Department of Human Services and trundled off to separate foster homes.

All of that could be avoided, of course, if the taxman would give me a break. But the government doesn't care that my father dropped all our mad money at *The Sweet Pickle* last month, paying off his bar tab before the owner's grandson, Hal, made good on his threat to beat the money out of Chuck. The taxman wants the delinquent taxes, and the kids, whose lives that measly twelve hundred dollars is going to ruin, be damned.

You'd have the cash if you'd stood up to Chuck and kept your mouth shut about where the money was hidden.

"Right," I mumble to myself. "And let a guy with a metal plate in his shoulder get beaten half to death."

"You talking to me, Caitlin?" Danny calls out from the living room, where my twelve-year-old brother has settled in to play one of his bloody video games while the baby is watching Sesame Street upstairs.

"No!" I shout. "And turn that down. I can't hear myself think."

Danny ups the volume in response. I grit my teeth and shift the electrical bill to the back of the queue—it's April and still cool, we can make do without air conditioning if the electricity gets shut off—but that only frees up another hundred and twenty bucks. I can snag a bag of groceries from Sister Maggie down at the church, but that won't feed this crew for more than a few days.

Three boys between the ages of eight and twelve take down a *lot* of food, and even Emilie is starting to put away her share. Emmie's always been on the small side so I'm glad she's putting on weight, but at the rate these kids are sucking down mac 'n cheese there's no way I'm paying the property tax without somebody going hungry. Unless a rich old aunt from the old country dies and leaves me her fortune, that twelve hundred, seventy-three dollars, and two cents I need by next Wednesday might as well be twelve million.

My gram always said you couldn't make a silk purse from a sow's ear, and I don't even have a sow's ear. I've got three little brothers, a two-year-old niece I've raised since she was two months old, a father who hasn't held down a job in six months, a hundred bucks left in my bank account, and bills.

To say this is not the way I was hoping to spend my twentieth birthday would be an understatement.

"Well, look at you." Daniel breezes into the kitchen, video game controller still in hand, to grab a fistful of pretzels from the bin on the counter. He munches as he looks me up and down, taking in my skintight black jeans and shimmering gold tank top with a curled lip. "Looking slutty. Where you going?"

"Out with Sherry," I say, with a glare. "And watch your mouth."

With his dark blonde curls, green eyes, and ski-slope nose, Danny and I resemble each other more than anyone else in the family, but we couldn't be more different. I spend my life cleaning up other people's messes; he spends his lighting fires for me to put out. He's a smart-mouthed troublemaker who's already made a name for himself with the Giffney P.D. and the only "bad" thing I've ever done was drop out of school when I was seventeen to take care of the baby and the other kids after my sister ran off. I work two jobs and do my best to make sure the kids eat healthy and Emmie doesn't watch too much T.V., while Danny is constantly on the verge of being suspended for conduct code infractions.

The chances of him graduating junior high, let alone high school, without a stint in juvie are looking less likely with every passing year, but still…I keep trying.

It's not like anyone else around here is going to be the voice of reason.

"Seriously, D," I say, knocking his hand away when he reaches for my Coke. It was the last one in the fridge and I need caffeine if I'm going to stay awake to celebrate my stupid birthday. "I don't want another call from Mr. Pitt. You need to pull it together and finish this year strong."

"Whatever." Daniel rolls his eyes. "Mr. Pitt can suck my dick."

"I'm serious, Danny." He reaches for my soda again and I slap his hand a second time. Harder. "No more language," I insist in my nag voice, the one I can barely stand to hear myself I've used it so much with him. "It's the straight and narrow for you. Even at home. I don't have time to deal with any more of your crap this month."

"What about your crap?" he mumbles. "You cuss all the time."

"Please, D..." I cross my arms and shake my head, too tired for the usual "but I'm an adult and I work my ass off to feed you so I can do what I want" lecture. "Can you give me a break? Just for a week or two? Until things calm down?"

He sighs, his lips pulling down at the edges as his gaze slides toward the envelopes spread out on the counter. "Everything's going to be okay though," he says, the sass gone out of his tone. "We're not going to lose the house, right?"

"Of course not," I lie, forcing a smile.

I refuse to let my brothers worry the way I've worried my entire life. One stomach full of acid and holes is enough for this family.

"I'm sorting it out," I continue, gathering the bills into a pile and shoving them back in the shoebox I keep on top of the fridge, wishing I could make our debt disappear as easily. "But if you've got any money left over from all that snow shoveling you did in January, it would help. I can pay you back once tips pick up at the restaurant."

Daniel shrugs. "You don't have to pay me back. I've only got forty bucks left, anyway. You can just take it."

"Thanks, booger." I smile, a real one this time, remembering why I couldn't have made it through parts of the past few years without this kid.

He's a pain in my ass, but he's also my right hand man when I need him.

"I love you," I say, ruffling his hair. "You know that, right?"

"Puke," Danny says, but there's a smile tugging at his lips when he lifts his hands into the air, warding off the hug he can no doubt sense is coming. "I'll go get the money, but you have to tell Ray to get out of the bathroom. I've been trying to get a shower since I got back from practice and he's been in the bath for a fucking hour and a half."

"Language!" I call out to my brother's retreating back. "And check Emmie's pull-up while you're upstairs."

"Whatever," Danny calls back, but I know he'll check.

He loves Emmie, probably more than he loves anyone in the world. Danny was a nine-year-old obsessed with monster trucks and boxing robots when our big sister, Aoife, left her daughter at our house and split. Nothing in Danny's nature up to that point had indicated a paternal streak, but he couldn't get enough of his baby niece. He carried Emmie all over the house, talking non-stop, and dragged her Pack 'n Play into his room so he could watch over her while she slept.

Even now, Emmie's toddler bed sits in the corner of Danny's room, her dolls, baby blocks, and pink toy kitchen a stark contrast to the skateboard posters and skeleton stickers decorating the other side of the room. It's Danny who Emmie crawls in bed with when she has a bad dream, and Danny who finally got her *mostly* potty-trained a few weeks back, saving me some much needed money on pull-ups.

The chances that Danny and Emmie will end up in the same foster home are slim to none. And even if they do, I can't imagine a foster family agreeing to a twelve-year-old boy and a two-year-old girl sharing a room. There are probably rules against that kind of thing, rules that have to be followed no matter how much it's going to devastate two kids who love each other.

My stomach gurgles and acid burns the back of my throat.

"You're going to figure it out," I mutter to myself, crossing to grab an antacid.

I'm on top of the kitchen counter on my knees, reaching up to the top shelf where I've kept the medicine since Ray ate a bar of chocolate laxatives when he was seven, when the front door opens and the smell of garlic and melted cheese wafts through the living room into the kitchen.

Immediately, my breath comes easier and my stomach gurgles—with hunger this time—reminding me I haven't eaten anything since ten o'clock this morning.

"Pizza!" Isaac booms in his relentlessly upbeat voice as the door slams shut behind him. "Come and get it, Cooneys!"

"You're an angel!" I call out, grinning as I hop down from the counter, antacid forgotten as I make a beeline around the island into the living room.

Footsteps thunder down the stairs, and moments later Isaac is surrounded by jumping kids, and four pairs of grabbing hands.

"Hold on," he says, holding the pizza out of Danny's reach, brown eyes crinkling at the edges when he laughs. "Wash your hands first. It's too hot to eat yet, anyway."

"Wash 'em good," I call out as Danny, Ray—who has apparently decided to emerge from bath time seclusion in the name of supper—and Sean race each other toward the downstairs bathroom.

I scoop Emmie up before she can get trampled and lean in to give Isaac a hug.

"Hey there." He squishes Emmie and me against a soft brown tee shirt that smells pleasantly of wood-fired pizza oven, pine-scented air freshener, and best friend. "How you holding up?"

"Pretty good," I say, melting into the hug.

Isaac's always been a big guy—he played football when we were in high school and at Limestone College until he quit to run the family pizza joint after his dad's stroke—but since he started working at *Frank's Pies*, he's acquired a tummy to go with the muscles. His girlfriend, Heather, teases him about it, but I kind of like the pudge. There's something comforting about hugging a guy who feels like a giant, cuddly bear, but is also capable of ripping a bad guy's head off with his bare hands.

"Pretty good, you think you've got the problem licked?" Isaac asks as he pulls away to set the pizza boxes balanced in his free hand on the crumb-covered table. "Or pretty good, you've only had seven antacids today instead of twelve?"

I wrinkle my nose, but am spared from answering when Danny skids to a stop beside me and dives for the pizza.

"Hold on a second! Let me get plates and napkins." I hurry into the kitchen, grabbing plates and the roll of paper towels and sliding them across the island to Isaac, who deals out place settings like a round of cards.

Emmie, still balanced on my hip, starts to squirm—obviously ready to join the big boys at the table—so I hurry over to the sink.

"Let's get your hands clean, doodle." I shift her around, balancing her between my body and the sink so our hands can tangle together beneath the cool stream of water.

I focus on her pudgy little fingers, wondering how I'm going to hold up without seeing them every day. Raising a baby and my younger brothers on my own for most of the past two and a half years has been so difficult and time-consuming there hasn't been much time to think.

No time to think about how they feel like *my* kids now, not Dad's or Mom's or—God forbid—my piece of shit sister's. No time to think about how much a part of me they are, how my world revolves around them, or how much I would miss the chaos and the laughter and the crazy and even the hard stuff if it were all to suddenly vanish.

This family has cost me my fair share of blood, sweat, and tears, but they are mine and I love them.

I need them. So fucking much.

CHAPTER 2

CAITLIN

"*I* think her hands are clean." The words come from over my shoulder, so close it feels like they're echoing inside my skull.

I jump and turn to see Isaac standing behind me, arms held out. It's only then that I realize Emmie's squirming has become fussing—or as close as she ever gets to fussing.

Emmie's always been quiet and small. Slow to walk, slower to talk, and always lagging in the pitiful percentiles on the charts the doctor fills out on her well-baby visits. But I don't pay attention to the pity in Dr. Naper's eyes when he talks about her developmental delays. Emmie is no dummy. I see her smarts in the clear blue eyes that look up at me when I scoop her up out of bed every morning. One day she's going to start talking a blue streak and make every doctor who ever threw around words like "fetal alcohol syndrome" eat their words. I believe that—believe in her—with my entire heart.

"No foster parent is going to know her like I do," I whisper, tears filling my eyes as I hand Emmie over to Isaac. "They won't fight for her, like I had to fight for Ray when that bitch, Mrs. Porter, wanted to flunk him after Mom left."

Isaac's forehead wrinkles, making him look like a sad puppy. "Let me get Emmie in her high chair," he says softly. "Stay here. I'll be right back."

I nod, rubbing the tears from my eyes with the backs of my fists, ashamed of myself. I don't cry. I don't have time, especially not now. I need to focus on pulling a solution out of my ass, not waste time whining about shit that hasn't even happened yet.

By the time Isaac comes back into the kitchen with two slices of pepperoni on a plate, my boo-hooing is over, replaced by the more familiar waves of acid lapping at the back of my throat. When he tries to hand over the pizza, I shake my head and hold up one hand. "I have to let the stomach volcano calm down first."

Isaac sets the plate on the counter where, moments before, I was playing Jenga with the bills. "That bad, huh?"

I nod, biting my lip, refusing to get emotional again. It's not going to do anyone any good, least of all the kids. "I've been over everything a hundred times. I just don't see how we can swing it."

"Well…" Isaac lets out a soft sigh as he leans against the counter beside me. "I've been thinking… I could give up my apartment and move back in with my parents. That would put me in a position to give you a loan."

I shake my head more emphatically. "No way. I won't let you do that. You and Ian would kill each other."

Ian, Isaac's little brother, is as big a waste of flesh as my sister. Ian did time for sexual assault—a rape he swore he didn't commit, but no one who knew him was surprised when he was found guilty. He's been crashing with his parents since he got out of jail, sitting on his ass for the better part of ten months, whining about how hard it is for a felon to get a job. Meanwhile, Isaac gave up getting his business degree to take over the pizza place, while Ian—who could have worked at his dad's restaurant, it's not like it was within two thousand feet of an elementary school or something—said he didn't have it in him to sweat over an oven after spending a year cooking for the other inmates at the state prison. And, incredibly, their mom humors the asshole, babying Ian while she leans on Isaac so hard it's a miracle he hasn't cracked under the pressure.

No, Isaac has enough on his plate. I can't let him take the kind of hit moving back in with his parents would deliver, not even for the kids.

"We wouldn't kill each other," Isaac says. "I might pound him into a bloody smear on the wall now and then, but...he'd survive. Most likely."

I smile. "And if he didn't, you'd go to prison, and

then whose couch would I crash on when I'm homeless?"

The humor vanishes from Isaac's expression. "You're not going to be homeless. We're going to figure this out, Caitlin."

"How?" I ask, pressing my lips together as I shake my head. "I can't let this shit drag anyone else down but…I can't see a way out. We're drowning, and I can't find a life boat, no matter where I look."

"It's going to be okay," Isaac says, cupping my face in his big hand, a gesture I know is meant to be comforting, but only makes me more aware of how small I am. I'm five feet three inches, in heels, and Dad always says I look like I'd blow away in a strong wind. I'm small, scrawny, and I've been fooling myself thinking I can hold everything together. The only thing to do now is to start preparing for the worst…or get so drunk I forget about all the problems for a night.

Getting wasted isn't usually my style—between my alcoholic mom and dad and druggie sister, I've seen enough substance abuse to know better—but right now a shot of whiskey is sounding pretty damned good. And hell, it *is* my twentieth birthday, and I've got a fake ID burning a hole in my purse. I'm practically obligated to get wasted.

I sniff and pull away from Isaac with a hard grin. "Grab me a couple of antacids from the top shelf, will ya? I need to get some food in my stomach before I get to the club."

"Good plan," Isaac says, letting the heavy stuff drop the way he always does.

It's one of the reasons he's still my friend when so many others have come and gone. Isaac knows when to leave things alone, when to turn a blind eye to my father passed out on the floor by the back door or ignore the fact that Emmie's running around the house with a bare bottom because we ran out of diapers. He knows when to offer advice, and when to just be there, making me feel less alone.

"Thanks for watching the kids so Sherry and I can go out," I say, chomping the antacids he drops into my palm and washing away the chalk taste with a gulp of Coke that sets my teeth fizzing.

"My pleasure." Isaac hands me the plate of pizza and watches with a smile as I inhale half a slice in three bites.

"And have fun tonight, okay?" he says. "All the shit will still be here in the morning."

"Don't I know it," I say wryly, shifting to check on the kids as I finish my first slice of pepperoni. Miraculously, no fights have broken out in the ten minutes I've dropped my guard. Thank God for pizza and plenty of it.

"I meant you should have a good time," Isaac says, chucking me on the shoulder. "You deserve a break. Have a few too many; stay out until the sun comes up. I'll make sure the kids are in bed by ten and don't burn the house down."

"And teeth need to be brushed," I say around a

LILI VALENTE

mouthful of pizza. "Especially Sean. He's been pulling that 'wet the toothbrush and stick it back in the cup without brushing' thing lately."

Isaac gives me a thumbs up.

"And make sure Emmie goes potty last thing before bed," I continue. "She's less likely to have an accident that way."

"Got it." Isaac nods.

"And don't let Danny play anything violent while the little ones are downstairs," I say, finishing my second slice and wiping my hands on the ratty dish-towel hanging by the oven. "Those zombie games give Sean and Emmie both nightmares. Sean says they don't, but he's lying. And don't let Ray take another bath. He's used up enough hot water for one day, but make sure Danny and Sean—"

I'm interrupted by a hard knock on the front door. Seconds later Sherry slams into the house with a whoop.

"What's up, people!" she calls out as she breezes through the living room.

She's wearing as few clothes as possible—black hot pants and a red halter top, paired with heels that look sharp enough to be used as a murder weapon—and her curly red hair is teased into a sexy mess that makes it clear she's prepared to party.

"Ready to jet, Cait?" she asks, wiggling her fingers at Isaac.

"Yes, she is." Isaac turns me around by the shoulders and walks me into the living room. "Get her out of here before she starts making lists."

18

I turn back to him, hands on my hips. "Do I need to make a list?"

"No!" Isaac and Sherry say at the same time.

"Isaac's got this. Let's go." Sherry grabs my hand and tows me toward the door. "We can get in free to *Elevation* if we get there before nine o'clock."

"In bed by ten, y'all," I call out to the kids as I grab my purse from the hook near the door. "And don't give Isaac any crap."

"Have fun!" Ray calls out.

"Happy Birthday, sissy, I love you," Sean says, earning my forgiveness for being a toothbrush-avoiding turd.

"Don't get pregnant," Danny adds, followed by a sharp, "Hey!" when Isaac thunks him on the back of the head.

"Have fun, ladies!" Isaac calls out, grinning as Danny tackles him and they both go rolling onto the carpet. By the time Sherry and I escape out the front door, Sean has launched himself onto the pig pile and all three of them are laughing like idiots.

I know the roughhousing will end in tears—it always does—but I resist the urge to head back into the house and put an end to the madness.

As of now, I'm officially off duty. For the next few hours, I'm not Caitlin the loyal daughter, Caitlin the responsible sister, or Caitlin the dutiful aunt. Tonight I'm going to be the Caitlin who knows how to let her hair down, who can dance all night and still have enough energy to hit the diner before sunrise. I'm ready to cut loose and have some fun before focusing my entire being on finding a way to keep things from going to rot and ruin.

I have no clue that this will be the night that changes everything, the night *he* sweeps into my life like a summer storm, washing away all those years of hard work and good intentions, making me someone different than I was before.

CHAPTER 3

GABE

"If music be the food of love, play on." –Shakespeare

The brunette next to me in the black leather booth overlooking the dance floor is going on and on about how much she enjoys volunteering at the battered women's shelter my mother and her DAR cronies fund as their pet project.

Shannon Griffon sits with her shapely, tanned legs demurely crossed, her curve-hugging—yet tasteful—beige dress tugged down to her knees. She extols the virtues of the brave women and adorable children who take refuge at the shelter in words as eloquent as her clothing, each sentence out of her mouth more heartwarming than the last, but all I keep thinking is that this is an hour of my life I'll never get back again.

An entire, precious hour wasted making small talk with a sweet, doe-eyed girl my mother insisted I take out for drinks, when I could be down on the dance floor with a woman who might actually be up for having a good time later tonight.

"Don't you think that's so important?" Shannon asks, raising her voice to be heard over the pulsing club beat. "I mean, I don't know what I'd do without a space of my own. I think every human being deserves that."

I nod lazily—hoping she'll wind down and I'll be able to make my excuses and head for the exit—but apparently even that small sign of interest is enough to convince Shannon I'm engaged. She launches into another monologue that I'm certain is sincere, not simply an attempt to impress her boss's son, but I don't care. I don't care that Shannon and I share a passion for righting societal wrongs. I don't care that Shannon is a perfectly nice person. I don't care that she has a good heart and a hot body and would probably make someone a great girlfriend.

That someone isn't me, and the sooner we both understand that, the better.

"I'm sorry," I say, interrupting her lecture on the importance of treating the poor with dignity. "I have to get going."

Shannon blinks. "Oh. Okay." She lets out a noise that is half sigh, half nervous laugh. "But we're having such a good time."

"No, we're not," I say, knowing honesty is the best way to make sure she gets the message, and my mother never tries to set me up with anyone, ever again. "You seem nice, Shannon, but I'm not interested. Not even a little."

Her jaw drops. "I… I can't believe you just said that."

I lift one shoulder. "I know. I'm rude. You're better off without a guy like me." I pat her bare knee, not surprised to feel nothing when I touch her, not even the slightest spark of attraction. "I'm sure you'll make some frat boy very happy when you go back to the university next fall."

Shannon surges to her feet, hair flying as she turns to go only to spin back when she realizes she's forgotten her purse. "You're a jerk, Gabe Alexander, and you can rot in heck for all I care," she says, the anger flashing in her brown eyes making her marginally more attractive.

But only marginally.

"Drive safe." I lift one hand and watch Shannon storm away, weaving in and out between the dark black booths lining the balcony, with the swiftness of a girl who drank virgin margaritas all night.

Virgin drinks with Mother Theresa. So far, this evening has been so G-rated it's left a saccharine taste in my mouth.

"Whiskey," I say to the cocktail waitress when she tries to drop off the check—mistakenly assuming I'll be leaving with my date. "Double. On the rocks. The best you've got."

She nods, setting the feathers on the ridiculous

hat *Elevation* makes its female staff wear bobbing before she walks away.

I settle back into the booth, the tension easing from my shoulders. I suppose some people might be more tense after pissing off their date, but I'm happy to have reclaimed my night. Shannon will be fine. I've done her a favor, really. Some girls have to be burned a few times before they wise up, get over their "saving the bad boy" fantasies, and go looking for a nice guy.

Bad boys are a waste of a woman's time. Most of us are past saving, and the rest have zero interest in Happily Ever After. Hell, I have zero interest in Happy For Now. I just want to feel alive, to look into a girl's eyes and see something that's going to keep my mind off all the things I refuse to think about for an hour or two.

The thought is barely through my head when I see *her*, the blonde in the gold tank top and the painted on jeans thrashing in the center of the dance floor below.

I smile, knowing my night is about to get a lot more interesting.

CHAPTER 4

GABE

The blonde dances like a woman possessed—arms up, head tossing from side to side, hair flying, hips swiveling with a sensual abandon that has the men surrounding her twisting their necks to get a better look at her ass, but she doesn't seem to realize she's causing a commotion.

Or if she does, she doesn't care. She isn't dancing for the people watching. This dance is about her and the music. She's feeding off every pulse of the bass, every eerie note the female singer croons about castles in the sky. The girl dances like this moment is all there is, all she needs, all she'll ever have, and I know right then—I have to have her.

A second later I've dumped forty dollars on the table and I'm out of my booth, moving smoothly down the circular staircase to the dance floor, my double shot of whiskey forgotten. I ease off the last step and head straight for my girl, not surprised when the men and women in my way sense me coming and instinctively shift out of my path.

Over the past few months, I've stopped giving a shit about almost everything and I've started fearing nothing. One thing I've learned in that time is that average folks are scared of people like me. Humans are hard-wired to possess a certain degree of fear. Fear keeps us safe from predators. Fear keeps us out of the path of oncoming traffic and our fingers out of the flames. People who aren't afraid are danger- ous, unpredictable, like a field full of landmines you're better off not trying to cross.

But I have a feeling my tiny dancer is the kind who enjoys danger.

I reach her as the bass line is escalating, thumping faster and faster, becoming a desperate, hungry pulse that fills the club and reverberates off the walls. Her hips keep time, wiggling in tight circles that make it impossible not to imagine her blond curls tumbling around her bare shoulders while she rides me, faster and faster until we both explode.

Judging by the expressions on the faces of the two meatheads in matching polos hovering behind her, the jocks were having similar thoughts, but when I move between them and the object of their desire, they step back. Their lizard brains can prob- ably tell picking a fight with me wouldn't end well, even if my biceps aren't the size of watermelons.

Not sparing my competition another thought, I shift my focus to the girl's flying hair and undulating hips and let go. I let go of everything—the residual irritation from the time I wasted with Shannon, the burning in my gut from my latest fight with my parents, the heavy gray weight of the undeniable things I drag around behind me every minute of every day, and the frustrated ambitions that hover around me like a poisonous fog. It all vanishes, leaving nothing but the girl and me and the music.

I've been dancing less than a minute when she turns—pivoting toward me and moving in close—and I know she's felt it, the draw of two like-minded creatures, a pull a hundred times more powerful than the opposing poles of a magnet.

Some may say opposites attract, but when it comes to human nature, like craves like.

My girl shifts closer, so close the hair flying around her face lashes the bare skin below the sleeves of my tee shirt, leaving a pleasant stinging sensation behind. The smell of her—cedar and soap and darker, smokier things—fills my head, ratcheting up my awareness. It's an unexpectedly masculine smell, but I like it. It suits her, somehow. She might be smaller than almost every other girl on the dance floor, but her ferocity is evident in every hip swivel, in every confident thrust of her thin arms into the air.

By the time she fists her hand in my shirt, pulling me to her, I'm already halfway to being hard. Her curves pressing against me finishes the job, but she doesn't pull away when my erection brushes against her belly. In fact—from what I can see of her pink lips between the flashing lights and the hair swirling around her face—I think she smiles.

A suspicion of a smile is enough for me to wrap my arm around her waist and lift her slim frame, shifting my jean-clad thigh between her legs.

She stiffens slightly as I urge her closer, until every roll of our hips sends my thigh into intimate connection with her heat. Her fingers claw into my shoulders and I catch a glimpse of her full bottom lip trapped between adorably jagged teeth. She sighs and throws her head back, giving me a glimpse of her pale throat and a jaw so delicate I could fit it in one hand.

Her head snaps back up a moment later, her hair flying around both our faces, and I feel the last of her resistance vanish. She gives in to the moment, to the music, to the way our bodies fit so perfectly together it's as if God made us to dry hump on the dance floor of the only semi-cool club in northern South Carolina.

I pull her closer, driving my fingers through her hair as our foreheads touch. Her nails dig into my skin so hard I can feel it through my tee shirt, her breath is warm and sweet against my lips, and the soft sound she makes as I tighten my fist in her hair is enough to make my skin go fever hot all over.

I suddenly can't wait another minute to be alone with her. The music that was fuel for the fire is now a giant gnat buzzing around my head, keeping me from being able to hear the sexy little breaths my girl is making as our dance gets progressively more erotic.

"Let's go somewhere," I say in her ear—perfect seashell ear so sweet looking I can't wait to trace each curve with my tongue. "Get out of here."

She shakes her head as she pulls away, giving me my first good look at her face. "I can't, I…" Her words cut off, replaced by a shocked expression I'm sure mirrors my own.

And I don't shock easily. Not any more.

But finding out the wild, uninhibited stranger, who's been grinding on my leg in public, is the most uptight good girl I've ever met—a girl so good she nuclear bombed her entire life to enable her ghetto family's bullshit—is shocking stuff.

Still, I recover before she does, and smile.

"Caitlin." I shout to be heard over the new song, a hip-hop number less pulsing than the techno number before it. "Haven't seen you in a while."

"You still haven't seen me," she says, swallowing hard. "This never happened."

I smile wider. "Oh, come on. You seemed to be enjoying yourself. I was. Sure you don't want to come back to my place?"

"No way in hell," she says, her mouth going tight around the edges, the way it did when she'd turn in her seat during study hall and demand that my friends and I shut up, because "some people need to get their homework done before work, assholes."

Back then, she was so uptight it was easy to

ignore how pretty she was, but now that I've seen her dance, smelled her intoxicating scent, and had her breasts flattened against my chest as she writhed against me, I don't want to ignore it. I don't want to let Caitlin walk away without finding out if there's more wild child hiding beneath her chilly exterior.

When she spins and hurries away without so much as a "fuck you," I follow, stalking her across the dance floor.

I'd never pursue a girl who legitimately had no interest, but I know Caitlin wants me, and I want to feel her fingernails digging into my shoulders again, this time with no clothes between us. I want to feel her breath hot on my lips as she calls my name when I make her come, and come, and come again, until neither of us can hold a thought in our heads and there is nothing in the world but how good it feels to fuck.

Hot, sticky, sweaty, no-holds-barred fucking until the sun rises tomorrow morning.

I have my share of addictions, but this is my drug of choice—the hunt, the rush as I see how fast I can get the woman of the night naked and willing. It usually doesn't take long. Ten minutes, fifteen— maybe an hour if she's one of those sweet, Southern types who still gives a shit if a guy thinks she's a "bad girl."

As far as I'm concerned, there is no such thing as a "bad girl," simply girls who've embraced their sexuality and refuse to feel shame about it, and those who haven't. But, if we *must* call women who like to come with a variety of consenting partners "bad girls," then I'm a fan.

Bad girls are one of my favorite things and—despite what I know of Caitlin's past—every second of that dance assured me she's my kind of woman. I'm the one pursuing her across the dance floor now, but I wouldn't be surprised to find myself handcuffed to her headboard by the end of the night.

In fact, I'd enjoy it.

CHAPTER 5

CAITLIN

"It's the first drop that destroys you, there's no harm at all in the last." –Irish proverb

Sherry is grinning as she leans into the bar —granting the bartender, who brought her band aids for her blisters, a better view of her cleavage—but her smile vanishes the moment she sees my face, confirming I must look as shaken as I feel.

"What's wrong?" she shouts, plunking back onto her stool hard enough to make her breasts threaten to bounce out of her top.

"Nothing." I shake my head. "I just want to get out of here."

"What?" Sherry squints, as if that will help her hear me.

It's quieter by the circular bar than out on the

dance floor, but still way too loud. Every thump of the bass rips through my head, pounding what's left of my brain, after I realized I was dirty dancing with Gabriel Alexander, to mush.

Fucking Gorgeous Gabe, one of the many privileged assholes I wasn't sorry to see the last of when I dropped out of Christoph Academy, kissing my scholarship goodbye. As far as actions went, Gabe wasn't particularly memorable. Sure he was spoiled, entitled, goofed off during study hall, and had no clue how hard most people have to work to scrape by, but he wasn't any more obnoxious than the other private school twerps.

No, what made Gabe stand out was how damned, crazy, stupid beautiful he was. The boy has cheekbones that would make a super model jealous, jagged brown hair that falls in edgy waves over his forehead, and piercing blue eyes so pale they seemed to glow, to burn with an icy fire that promises wicked and delightful things. And the rest of him is nothing to sneeze at either. Even back in high school, he had a body that inspired giddy, heart-littered graffiti in the girls' bathroom, but now...

Now, he is sex in two-hundred dollar blue jeans. He is built like an athlete and moves like an animal, so completely uninhibited it makes even me feel reserved in comparison. *Me*, who doesn't have a shy bone in her body when it comes time to hit the dance floor.

I never feel more alive than when I'm dancing. If

I weren't juggling two jobs and have kids to take care of, I'd be at a club every night. Dancing is my drug, my rush, the only thing that takes me out of my head and connects me to that deep, primal part of myself I keep locked away most of the time.

And, up until tonight, it was something I preferred to do alone. Sure, I'll dance with a guy now and then, but nothing like what happened with Gabe. That dance was soul-shaking, panty-melting, so damned sexy my skin is still buzzing and my heart racing and my stomach feels like it's turning inside out. I can't remember the last time I felt this way—if I've *ever* felt this way—or wanted someone the way I want Gabe.

If I don't get out of the club ASAP, I know I'll do something I'll regret.

Going home with a guy isn't on the agenda, but especially not a guy like Gabe. I don't have room in my life for a smug, privileged asshole who probably spends more money per month on carwashes than I do on groceries to feed a family of six. Not now, when everything at home is falling apart and I'm feeling the difference between a person like me and a person like Gabe more keenly than I ever have before.

"Come on." I tug on Sherry's arm, pulling her off her stool. "Let's go."

She nods and holds up one finger before leaning over the bar to say goodbye to the bartender she's been flirting with all night. I turn, scanning the club for six feet of walking sex appeal, but thankfully,

Gabe is nowhere to be seen. Sherry and I make it up the stairs and through the front lobby into the street without running into any trouble, and my chest loosens in relief.

"Let me go get the car," I say, holding out my hand for her keys as she limps to the curb beside me. "That way you won't make your blisters any worse."

"Uh-uh," Sherry says. "You've been drinking. I'll take my shoes off and go barefoot."

I shake my head. "There's broken glass and cigarette butts and a hundred other nasty things between here and where we're parked. I had my second whiskey sour two hours ago; I'm fine to drive. Hand over the keys, I don't want you getting hurt."

"Yes, ma'am." Sherry rolls her eyes as she drops the keys in my hand. "You're such a mom, sometimes."

"All the time," I counter with a grin. "Be right back."

You weren't acting like a mom ten minutes ago, I think, as I turn to go, my gold, high-heeled sandals clicking on the sidewalk.

No, I wasn't, and that scares me as much as the fluttery feeling still filling my chest. I can't afford to lose control, even for a night. I'm all my brothers and Emmie have left. I can't let them down. I don't have time for distractions like Gorgeous Gabe. Between working five lunch shifts a week at *Harry's* and almost every Friday and Saturday night at the movie theater, I barely have time to make sure the kids are fed, bathed, homework done, doctor appointments kept, Danny's latest school crisis averted, and a couple of loads of laundry done per week.

I don't have room in my life for a boyfriend and I don't do one-night stands. Before my big sister skipped town, she made sure the name "Cooney" was synonymous with "easy lay"—I've been called a slut behind my back since long before I ever kissed a guy—but despite the gossip around the neighborhood, this Cooney sister isn't into casual hook-ups. Not that I think they're wrong, or that I wouldn't enjoy making out with one of Isaac's beefy football player friends or the notoriously hot Lombardi boys down the street.

My problem is that I'm pretty sure I'd enjoy it too much. It would be so easy to get addicted to a feeling as electric as what I felt in Gabe's arms, so easy to forget all the lives depending on me and get lost in that hunger, lost in him.

"Don't think about it," I say aloud, earning myself a sideways glance from the two college boys in brightly colored polo-shirts walking in the opposite direction, making me realize how long it's been since I've stepped out of my routine.

At home and at both of my jobs, everyone knows I talk to myself. It's something that's taken for granted, as much a part of me as my green eyes or the scattering of freckles across my nose. No one bats an eye when I walk around the restaurant mumbling my to-do list, but in the real world, people think girls who talk to themselves are crazy.

And maybe I *am* crazy, because when I pull up in front of the club and see Gabe standing next to Sherry—nodding seriously as my best friend talks a mile a minute—a shockwave of pleasure shoots through me.

I'm happy to see him. Very happy.

Which is *bad*, so bad, and likely to get worse if the determined look in Gabe's piercing blue eyes is anything to judge by.

CHAPTER 6

CAITLIN

swallow, ignoring the way my heart beats in my throat as I roll down the passenger's window and call for Sherry to get in.

"Hey." She leans down, a guilty-excited look on her face that makes me even more uneasy. "I've decided to take a cab. I should get home and put some medicine on my blisters, but you and Gabe can have the car."

My brows draw together so swiftly my head jerks. "What?"

"We're taking the car," Gabe says as he eases around Sherry.

Before I can hit the lock button, he's inside the vehicle, settling into the seat next to me, filling the cab of Sherry's VW Bug with that clean-dirty smell of his. Clean, because the soapy scent that clings to his skin speaks of long showers and luxury bath products and other sensual things; dirty, because the base note of man and spice and sex that hovers around Gabe is enough to make my mouth water, to make me want to give in the way I gave in on the dance floor and let him take control.

"Get out," I mutter through gritted teeth, shooting him my most serious glare, the one that makes Danny jump up from his video games and set the table without a hint of backtalk.

I need Gabe out of this car—now.

"No," he says, making my jaw clench harder. "I'm going to help you get what you need."

"I don't need your help," I say with a huff, insulted that he's reduced sleeping with me to an act of pity. "I'm not anyone's charity case, certainly not yours."

"I know that." Gabe nods, but makes no move to exit the car. "That's why I'm going to *help* you get what you need, instead of giving it to you. Charity can be insulting, no matter how well-intentioned, and I think we'll both have more fun this way."

"What are you talking about?" I ask, no longer certain this conversation is about sex.

"Your friend told me about the property taxes," he says. "I know where we can get the money."

My mouth falls open, but before I can recover Sherry breaks in.

"Okay, well you two have fun." She wiggles her fingers as she backs away from the car, the giddy look on her face making it clear she thinks she's doing me a favor by throwing me to the wolves.

To one wolf, anyway, one who watches me with

cool blue eyes that make my lips prickle as his gaze lingers on my face.

"I'll swing by your place tomorrow morning and pick up the car," Sherry continues as she hops back onto the sidewalk to await her taxi. "Do all the things I wish I was doing tonight. At least twice!"

"I'm going to kill you," I say, ignoring the heat that flushes my face.

"Sounds good." She giggles, obviously not taking my threat seriously.

But she's right, of course. I'm not going to kill her, or even hold a grudge for more than a day. I can't stay mad at Sherry. She's impulsive and crazy and runs her mouth when she shouldn't, but she's been my friend since third grade.

She and Isaac were the only friends who didn't lose interest when I got an academic scholarship to Christoph Academy and switched high schools. They were also the only ones who came by to visit me when I quit the academy to stay home with Emmie.

Sherry was my rock, stopping by the store for more diapers when Emmie was too sick for me to take her out and keeping me company when the stress of caring for an infant and three wild boys threatened to unravel what was left of my sanity. Back then, I'd been so overwhelmed I couldn't have imagined things getting any harder, but they had. And I had survived, the way I always do—on my own, without any handouts or knights in shining BMWs.

I have no idea what kind of "help" Gabe plans on shelling out, but I know I want no part of it.

"Should I drop you off at your car?" I ask as I pull back onto the road. "Or do you need a ride home?"

"We're going to the corner of Grant and Hawthorne," Gabe says. "Do you know where that is?"

I grunt beneath my breath. "That's my side of town."

"Is it?" he asks, as if he doesn't know I live on the wrong side of the tracks—both sets of them. "Then I assume you know how to get there."

"I do, but—"

"Good, but don't drive past the pawnshop on the corner," he interrupts. "You'll want to park before we get there, preferably on a side street." He reaches down, releasing the seat handle and scooting back to make more room for his long legs—his thickly muscled, long legs, one of which was between my thighs less than an hour ago when we were grinding on the dance floor.

I take a deep breath in and let it out slowly through my nose, fighting the memory and the sizzle of awareness it generates.

"Listen, I appreciate that you'd like to help," I say. "But I don't have anything worth pawning and I don't want your money."

"I'm not giving you my money, and we won't be pawning anything," he says, his voice low, silky smooth, and as ridiculously sexy as everything else about the man Gabe's become. "The shop is closed. The owner's spending some time in the hospital after being hit in the head with a baseball bat."

"Crap," I say, forehead wrinkling. "Poor guy."

"Don't waste your pity." Gabe leans back in his seat as I guide the bug down Limestone Avenue and take a right near the courthouse. "Mr. Purdue broke his wife's arm in three places and cracked two of her ribs before his daughter hit him with the baseball bat, knocking him out long enough to get her mother out of the house alive."

My eyes go round and my stomach lurches. "How do you know that?"

"My father is Mr. Purdue's defense attorney," he says. "I'm working at the office while I'm taking a semester off. I read the case file. It had all the gory details."

I peek at him, dividing my attention between him and the road. "You're kidding right?"

"I'm not." Gabe sighs and for the first time I see a crack in his cool, confident exterior. I can tell he hates that his dad is representing a man who would beat his wife. "But Dad will defend any scumbag with enough cash to pay his retainer, and he's the best, so there's a good chance Mr. Purdue will get off. Assuming his wife's courage holds, of course, and she doesn't change her mind and refuse to testify the way she did last time."

I shake my head, not knowing what to say. "Well, I guess everyone has the right to an attorney."

"They shouldn't," Gabe says, his voice hard. "Evil

people have too much protection under the law. It's the innocent who suffer while they try to prove they've been victimized. If you play by the rules, you get screwed. Every time."

I chew the corner of my lip, wishing I could disagree with him. But the system popped my optimistic cherry a long time ago, the year I spent three months in a foster home. The place was ten times worse than the house my caseworker plucked me out of, and I was stuck there for months while Chuck and my scatterbrained mom tried to follow all the rules to reestablish custody.

There had been three other foster kids in the house, and we'd passed around lice so many times I had to have my head shaved to get rid of it. Our foster mom gave me the crew cut herself. She couldn't be bothered to do all the washing and cleaning to get rid of the infestation, and I think a part of the sadistic bitch had enjoyed shaving off my waist-length hair. It had been so beautiful and healthy and shiny, the only part of my appearance I took pride in back when I was so skinny the kids at school made fun of the way my knobby elbows and knees stuck out from the rest of me.

I'd gone back home looking like a cancer patient. The moment my mom saw me, she'd burst into tears and run to her room, refusing to come out for the "welcome home" burgers and fries my dad had sprung for from McDonald's.

I should have known right then she wasn't in the motherhood game for the long haul. There is nothing that would keep me from hugging one of my kids if they'd been gone for three months. Nothing.

"That's why sometimes rules need to be broken," Gabe continues, pulling me from my thoughts. "Sometimes you have to take justice into your own hands."

I brake behind a row of cars already stopped at a red light and turn to face him, grateful for the chance to look him in the eyes. "Where are we going?" I ask, stomach gurgling with nerves. "What is this?"

His focus slides my way, the intensity in his expression enough to make me shiver. "We're going to get the money you need to keep your home and take care of your family."

"How?" I ask.

"You've already sacrificed your life on the altar of sisterly duty," he says, ignoring my question. "I'd hate to think all of that was for nothing."

"Keep your smartass comments to yourself," I say, gripping the steering wheel so tight my knuckles start to ache. "Or you can get out right here."

"I'm not being a smartass," he says, a gentle note in his voice that's almost as unnerving as his pene-trating stare. "I heard the gossip after you left school. You dropped out to take care of your brothers and niece because your dad's an alcoholic and your sister bailed on her kid, right?"

"Yeah. So?" I turn my attention to the road as the

cars begin to move, grateful for an excuse to break the eye contact that's making my skin feel too tight.

"Well, it isn't hard to read the writing on *that* wall," he says. "With four kids to feed, no diploma, no time or money for your own education, and no support from your family, there's no way you're getting out. Unless you dump the dead weight and let the state take the children, but you don't seem like the type." He pauses, cranking his window down a few inches, letting cool air and the smell of the honeysuckle starting to bloom beside the road rush into the car. "Unless something changes, you're headed down a long, hard road, with your chances of creeping above the poverty line ranging from slim to none."

I swallow, ignoring the lump in my throat, hating his prophecy, hating even more that it's already coming true. I haven't even had time to get my GED, let alone start college. I'll never make my dreams of getting a degree a reality, not when I have to work fifty hours a week just to keep food on the table.

"It's not your fault," he says, again in that kind way that sort of makes me want to punch him. "Like I said, the system is rigged. America isn't the land of opportunity, not anymore. It's a place where the rich get richer, and the poor get to watch reality television on increasingly affordable electronics."

"You think you're pretty clever, don't you?"

"I'm not clever, I'm realistic," he says. "I give my share to charity, but even if I gave my trust fund away, it wouldn't change a flawed system. Facts are facts, and the only way that certain people can break out is to stop playing by the rules and start playing to win."

He lifts a hand, pointing to the next turn onto Orchard Street. "Pull over up here and go around the block. We can park at the end of the street and sneak in through the back."

I take the turn onto Orchard, but instead of going around the block, I pull to the side of the road and shove the car into park.

"Sneak into where?" I ask, gut churning because I have a feeling I already know the answer. "What the hell are we doing, Gabe?"

"We're tipping the scales of justice in your favor with a little breaking and entering." His smile is so pleasant you'd think we were discussing the score of the latest RiverDogs game. "Sounds good, right?"

I shake my head. "No it doesn't. Not even a little bit." But even I can hear the uncertainty at the core of my words, gooey like a rotten nougat center.

How else am I going to get my hands on the kind of money I need before it's too late? Maybe Gabe is right, maybe there is only one way out for someone like me.

And maybe Mr. Purdue deserves whatever he gets...

"I can't," I say, heart racing. The voice in my head is seductive, but this isn't me. I've never stolen anything in my entire life. But then, I've never known the person I was planning to steal from was a monster, either...

"You can," Gabe says, a smile in his voice. "I know you have it in you. I saw it on the dance floor."

"No." I press my lips together. "I'm not that kind of person."

"Sometimes we don't know what kind of person we are until we're put into an impossible situation," Gabe says. "Situations that force us to think about what matters, and what's the best thing we can do with our lives in the time we're given. To me, taking care of your family seems a lot more important than obeying a law that says you can't steal from a fucking evil bastard."

I pull in a breath and let it out in a rush. I can't believe how much sense he's making.

The good girl in me still wants to turn my back on temptation and walk away from all this on principle, but my gut is screaming that principles have never gotten me anywhere. I can't afford principles, and why am I fighting to resist something that doesn't feel wrong in the first place?

"Come on, Cooney." Gabe brushes my hair behind my ear and I prickle all over, like my entire body is a sleeping limb struggling to come fully awake. "Let me help you get what you need."

What I need.

The way he says it, it's about so much more than money. It's about the way he makes my skin hot and my lips tingle, it's about the way he makes my heart race and banishes the exhaustion that's been my constant companion since I quit school to be a full-time surrogate parent. It's about the flicker of hope he lights inside me. That flame isn't much bigger than a candle right now, but I can sense how easy it would be for it to grow, to rise higher and higher until it sets my world on fire.

I'm standing at the threshold of a moment that will change my life, and not necessarily for the better. I know that, I know it with everything in me, all the way down to the marrow of my bones.

But still I nod.

And take his hand.

And let him lead me out into the night.

CHAPTER 7

GABE

"There is nothing either good or bad, but thinking makes it so." –Shakespeare

Television sets flicker behind living room curtains and loud laughter echoes down the street from a party further up the block as we make our way down Hawthorne Street, but no one sees the two silhouettes moving swiftly through the shadows beneath the broken streetlights.

Caitlin walks silently along beside me, a full two inches shorter now that she's slipped into a pair of tennis shoes we found in the Bug's trunk. She's so petite that the top of her head barely reaches the middle of my arm. I don't usually go for short girls —too hard to make six foot one and five foot one match up in certain situations—but I've decided to make an exception in her case.

All kinds of exceptions. Breaking all the rules of engagement tonight...but what else are rules good for?

I smile, grateful Caitlin can't see my face in the darkness. I know she's scared—any sane person would be; we're about to commit a felony—and I don't want her to realize how little this bothers me. I'm not a sociopath, at least not in the true sense, but she doesn't know me well enough to understand that it took a lot of time and thought for me to come to peace with breaking the law. She might be spooked by the smile and rethink her decision, and I don't want her to bail. I've never had an accomplice before, but I can already tell that crime is more fun when shared with someone special.

And Caitlin is special. She's fierce and shy, hard and kind, wild and domesticated, all at the same time. I was too stupid to appreciate someone like her back when we were in high school, but now I'm intrigued by her contradictions, and even more curious to see how she'll perform under pressure.

"How are we getting over?" Caitlin whispers as we stop beside the chain link fence surrounding the back of the pawnshop.

On the other side, the innards of rusted out machinery, old refrigerators, and a variety of battered bikes and once brightly-colored kids toys litter the hard-packed earth, belying the quality of the goods inside the store. But I know this isn't your average second hand junk store. Mr. Purdue has a thriving business to lose if he goes to jail. There is good money to be had within those crumbling brick walls and Caitlin and I are going to take our share of it.

"We'll climb over," I say, stripping off my shirt. "I'll go first and leave this on top of the barbed wire so you won't cut yourself."

Caitlin takes a shaky breath. "Are you sure you're going to be able to pick the lock? What if they have a security system?"

"Does this look like the kind of place that has a security system?" I begin to climb, knowing it's best not to give Caitlin too much time to think.

"I don't know," she whispers. "But what if it does?"

"Then we'll climb faster on the way out." I lay my shirt on the barbed wire at the top of the fence and swing a leg over to the other side. I doubt the Giffney P.D. will bother to check the fence for bloodstains, but best to be safe. There will come a day when I won't care if I'm caught, but that day hasn't arrived yet.

By the time I step down onto the ground, Caitlin is maneuvering over the barbed wire at the top of the fence. She has a harder time—her legs aren't as long and she ends up grabbing on to part of the tee-shirt-covered wire for balance—but she makes it over without cutting herself and starts swiftly down the other side. I stand watching her, head tilted back, wishing the moonlight was stronger so I could get a better look at the no-doubt delicious view of her jean clad ass.

As soon as she's within reach, I wrap my hands

around her waist and lift her the rest of the way down.

"I've got it," she says, brushing my hands away with a sharp exhale before stepping out of my arms.

"Don't be nervous," I say. "But don't touch anything. You're not wearing gloves and you'll leave prints."

"What about you?" she asks, following me across the junk-littered enclosure.

"I'll find something inside to wipe the knobs down on our way out." I pull my wallet from my back pocket and fetch my pick set from inside. "But even if I miss something, it's better my prints are found than yours. I have a lawyer in the family."

"All I have is crazy in mine," she mutters, crossing her arms and huddling close to my side, casting anxious glances around the yard as I go to work. "I always thought the gene skipped me, but now…" She shivers, despite the balmy early April night. "I can't believe I'm doing this."

"Everyone has crazy in their family," I say, slipping my tension wrench into the bottom of the keyhole. "And you're not being crazy, you're being brave."

She shakes her head. "I'm still not sure this is right, no matter what a waste this guy is."

"Would you say you have a well-developed sense of right and wrong?" I tease my pick into the lock above the tension wrench, raking it back and forth, getting a feel for the pins. There are five, maybe six.

It isn't a complicated lock. We should be inside in five minutes, maybe less.

"I think so," she says. "I mean, considering the way I was raised, I think my conscience is probably in better working condition than most people with parents like mine."

"Dad and Mom not the best role models?" I find the stubborn pin—the one I need to set first before I can move on to the others—and lean in, listening for the faint click that will let me know it has slid into place.

"My dad's a drunk, but he tries…or he used to, anyway. And my mom wasn't a bad person, just a flake and anxious all the time," Caitlin whispers quickly, making me think she's a little anxious herself. "She was okay when she was drinking, but once she got clean she couldn't handle all the noise and the chaos at the house. She ran off with her AA sponsor the day after she got her one month sobriety chip."

I grunt in amusement. "I always knew AA was bad news."

"Driving mothers away from their obnoxious children since nineteen thirty-five," she says with a soft laugh.

"I like that you laugh about it."

"It's either laugh or cry," she says, bumping my admiration for her up a notch, making me even more certain that I want to help her.

The thought of Caitlin getting kicked out of her house after all she's done to hold her family together sets my teeth on edge. The second her friend explained why Caitlin wasn't in the mood for partying, I resolved to make her problems go away.

I have fifty grand in my checking account and could get my hands on more if I wanted to—my grandmother removed the age restrictions on my inheritance a few months ago, so the sky is pretty much the limit. I could have given Caitlin the cash as an anonymous gift, but I'd already planned to hit Mr. Purdue's place sometime this week and couldn't resist the urge to kill two birds with one stone.

Besides, a shared secret brings people together, and eliminating Caitlin's money troubles will free her up to get into other kinds of trouble.

Trouble with me.

I hear the final pin click and my mouth fills with a sweet, electric taste. It's the taste of victory and forbidden things, two of the best tastes in the world.

I turn the tension wrench to the right and the door swings open.

"We're in?" Caitlin grabs my arm, her fingernails digging into my skin.

"We're in," I say, marveling that even that simple touch is enough to make me thicker.

This girl does something to me, something I can't wait to explore further…as soon as we get what we've come for.

"Let me check for an alarm." I move inside, scanning the walls on either side of the long, dark hallway. I don't see any control panels or flashing lights, and no cameras visible near the ceiling—not that anyone watching security footage would be able to make out our faces in the near-darkness, anyway.

I motion for Caitlin to follow, and we move down the hall, through a pair of swinging wooden doors, and into the main portion of the pawnshop without making a sound. Her steps are even softer than mine and I've had enough practice that I move like a ghost, barely touching the floor beneath me.

"Are you going to try the register?" she whispers as we stop behind the display cases.

I shake my head. "I doubt there will be any money in it. I'm going straight for the safe, see if I can get lucky."

"I'll find the keys to the display case and clean out the jewelry," she says, grabbing several tissues from a box on the back counter, taking my warning not to touch anything with bare hands to heart. "That's the most valuable small stuff. I can put it in my pockets, and I won't have to try to carry anything while I'm climbing back over the fence."

"Brilliant," I say, with a wink. "You're a natural."

"Say that after we get out of here without getting caught." She takes a deep breath in and out. "Because right now I feel like I'm about to throw up."

"Don't throw up." I squat beside the safe. "They might decide to test it for DNA."

"Is there DNA in vomit?"

I give the lock an experimental turn, pleased

when it sticks in one place. "Yes. In the cells from your stomach lining and your saliva."

She hums thoughtfully, the keys to the display case tinkling as she pulls them from a hook near the register. "But they'd have to have something to match the sample with, right? And I'm not in the police database."

"Let's keep it that way." I grab my own fistful of tissues. "In and out in ten minutes or less. That's my rule. Fill your pockets. I'll give the safe five minutes and if I can't get it open we'll get out of here."

"All right," she agrees.

I hear her moving around behind me and glass doors sliding open, but after only a few moments I lose awareness of anything but the subtle gumminess of the safe's dial near numbers sixty-three and the soft hitch in the rhythm near numbers fourteen and seven. I spin the digits from lowest to highest and back again. I try two more combinations with no luck, but on the third the safe pops open with a satisfying *thu-gunk*.

"Thank you, Mr. Purdue," I whisper, grinning as I pull stacks of rubber-band-wrapped bills from the safe and shove them into my back pockets.

"You did it?" Caitlin asks in an awed voice as she crouches down next to me. "Jesus Christ, you're a full-fledged criminal, aren't you?"

"Sometimes." I lean my face closer to hers, unable to resist the urge to flirt…just a little. "Want to play Bonnie and Clyde?"

Her green eyes widen. "Bonnie and Clyde killed people."

"Robin Hood and Maid Marian, then," I say, my lips only a breath away from hers, close enough to smell the sweet-and-sour candy scent of her breath and the wild spice of her perfume. I'm a chin tilt away from stealing a first kiss to go with the stacks of bills tucked into my pockets, when I hear muffled voices from the sidewalk outside the shop.

"Who's that?" Caitlin hisses, eyes flying wider. "Mr. Purdue?"

I shake my head, the hair at the back of my neck lifting as I pinpoint two, distinct male voices conversing in furtive tones. "I imagine it's—"

Before I can finish my sentence—or encourage Caitlin to start moving her sweet ass toward the exit—the sound of shattering glass slices through the silence, followed closely by the blare of an alarm.

I lift my hands to shove Caitlin toward the back door, but she's already on the move, darting out behind the display cases and booking it down the hall.

"Holy fuck, man, somebody's already in here!" a male voice shouts behind me as I follow Caitlin's lead.

When the first gunshot rings out, I'm already shoving the back door closed behind me, wiping it clean with the tissues in my fist, and sprinting across the yard. My footsteps pound the hard-packed dirt, eating up the ground with adrenaline-fueled swiftness. By the time the fence comes into view, Caitlin is already at the top, swinging her leg over the barbed wire.

My chest loosens with relief—she's going to make it out, even if I get shot in the back before I can follow. But I don't plan on getting shot, not if I can help it. Four feet from the fence, I jump, making it halfway up before my hands claw into the ribbons of metal and I begin to climb.

Unfortunately, my impact sends Caitlin flying off the other side, her heels hitting the dirt before her momentum carries her back onto her ass.

"Sorry!" I take the rest of the fence in three pulls of my arms and swing over, snagging my shirt off the barbed wire before leaping down to the ground beside her, landing with a grunt.

"Were those gunshots?" she asks, scrambling to her feet and grabbing my hand, obviously not in the mood to waste time with apologies.

"They were." I take off at a sprint, pulling her along with me. "And there will be sirens soon. Best if we're back in the car before then."

Seconds later, sirens wail in the distance.

Caitlin and I pick up our pace, reaching the dark corner where she parked the car in record time and slamming inside. Seconds later, she has the Bug started and rumbling down Orchard Street to the south headed toward Caffey Parkway and the highway, moving swiftly away from the sirens approaching from downtown.

66

"Fuck," Caitlin says, voice shaking. "Holy shit-fuck."

I laugh. "Aren't you glad we parked headed south," I say, breath still coming fast as I empty my pockets, shoving the money into a plastic bag I find on the floor.

"Fuck, Gabe," she says, louder this time. "We could have been shot!"

"But we weren't." I finish emptying my pockets and mop the sweat from my face with my tee shirt. "You're doing great, by the way. Two miles over the limit is perfect. Least suspicious speed there is."

"You're crazy." She shoves her hair from her face with a shaking hand. "I can't believe I let you talk me into this. What would have happened if I'd died? What would have happened to the kids?"

"The same thing that was going to happen if you didn't pay the property tax," I say logically. "They would have gone to foster homes. As far as the kids are concerned, the risk made sense. And this time, you gambled and won."

She shakes her head, but when she exhales the breath is smoother, longer.

"Can you empty your pockets while you drive?" I ask. "On the off chance we get cops on our tail and I need to throw this out the window, I want everything in one bag. I'll wipe your prints off the jewelry before I put it in."

Caitlin reaches into her front pocket, pulling out two nice watches and a pair of diamond studs before moving on to her back pockets. By the time she's done, my cupped hand is overflowing and I'm estimating another grand has been added to our stash.

"These are good," I say, wiping each piece before dropping it into the bag. "You snagged quality stuff."

"Is it enough to pay the taxes?" she mumbles. "That's all I want to know."

"I won't know for sure how much until I run it through my fence in Charleston, but I'd say a grand, easy. Until then, the cash from the safe should tide you over. I'll drop it by your place as soon as I check the serial numbers and make sure the bills are clean." I lean forward, seeing the muted lights of a city bus stop glowing on the corner up ahead. "Pull over up there. I'll get out and take the bus."

"You're not taking the bus," she says. "I'll take you home."

"Pull over," I insist. "The longer I stay in the car, the better the chances of you getting caught with stolen goods in your possession."

"So you'd rather have the stolen goods in *your* possession?" she asks, shooting me a narrow look. "You do plan on dropping off my share, right?"

"I plan on dropping off every penny," I say. "Now pull over."

"I'm not an idiot, Gabe." She slows, pulling to the side of the road beneath two ancient oak trees leaning over the street and cutting the lights before she turns to me. "People screw other people over. It's the way the world works. My mother took our grocery money with her when she left, and my sister took my car and left me with a kid to raise. You can't trust *family* with money, let alone some guy you barely know."

She straightens, lifting her chin and doing her best to look down her nose at me. "So I'd like my cut of the money now. Forty percent."

"You'll get one hundred percent, once I make sure the money is untraceable," I say, making no move to hand over the cash, needing her to know I'm not the type who follows orders. From anyone. Even girls I like as much as I'm coming to like her. "I have enough money to buy and sell your entire family. Twice. Money doesn't interest me, or have anything to do with what I want from you."

Her glare intensifies but I can see curiosity spark in her eyes. "So what do you want from me? Everybody wants something"

CHAPTER 8

GABE

"I want to get naked with you," I say, capturing a strand of her silky hair and twining it around my finger. "I want to taste your mouth and your skin and those inches between your legs you were grinding against me tonight. I want to hear you call my name when you come, and I want to see if you come the way you dance."

Even in the dim light I can see her throat work as she swallows. "I'm not a whore."

"I'm not asking you to be." I lean closer, tugging on my captive strand of hair, reeling her in. "We'll fuck because we enjoy it. Just like we enjoyed robbing that store tonight."

"I didn't enjoy it," she says softly, so close I can feel the air stir against my lips as she speaks. "I was scared to death."

"Liar," I whisper. "I bet you haven't felt that alive in years."

LILI VALENTE

"You're crazy," she says, breath coming faster as the tip of my nose brushes hers.

"I bet your skin is still tingling all over."

She makes a non-committal sound that becomes a sexy little sigh as I press a kiss to her cheek.

"And I bet if I slid my hand inside your panties they'd be wet," I whisper, biting back a groan as she squirms in her seat, thighs squeezing together before spreading in a silent invitation. "What do you think? Should I check?"

"Fuck you," she says.

I decide to take that as a yes.

I seal my lips over hers, moaning as I taste her for the first time and find her even more delicious than I expected. She tastes like rain and salt and the first bite of a peach, so sweet I'm suddenly starving for more of her, all of her.

I claim her mouth with deep strokes of my tongue, things low in my body twisting as she responds with hungry swirls of her own, pushing closer, deeper, until our teeth grind together through our lips and my cock strains the fly of my jeans and the need to see if she's as fucking turned on as I am grows too strong to resist.

I reach for the close of her jeans, ripping the button free with a sharp jerk that draws a surprised sound from the back of Caitlin's throat. But the moment my hand slides down the front of her panties, the sound becomes a hiss of breath and then a sigh as my fingers tease through her slick folds.

72

Damn, she's wet, as wet as I'd hoped she'd be. Wet and hot and silky soft, and there is nothing I want more in the world than to be inside her, to feel my cock gliding in and out of all that sweet heat. I want to fuck her until the world melts, until we both fall apart and come back together in each other's arms, and I want to stay in her arms after the fucking is over, if only to prove to her that some people do stick around.

At least for a little while.

"Stop," she mumbles against my lips, so I do, stilling with my middle finger up to the knuckle in her pussy.

"Please," she says, breath still coming faster. "Please, stop."

"I have stopped. I'll stop anytime you tell me to," I say, kissing her with the words, sealing the promise with a sweep of my tongue across her upper lip.

"I meant…this." She brings trembling hands to my arm and wraps her fingers around my wrist. But she doesn't pull me away, and her body lets out another delicious rush of heat, a rush that dampens my finger and makes my cock so hard it threatens to burst through denim to get to the girl sitting next to me.

"Are you sure you want me to stop?" I kiss my way down her throat, pulling my finger out until only the tip remains inside her. "Or are you just afraid of how far you want me to go?" I drive back inside, using two fingers this time, drawing a groan from Caitlin's throat that is raw and hungry and sexy as hell.

"And go and go," I whisper against her neck, picking up the pace of my thrusts. "And keep going until you beg me *not* to stop?"

Her breath catches as I add a third finger, stretching her slick channel as I rub the heel of my hand against the top of her, rubbing her clit in increasingly firm circles, waiting until she's clinging to my arms with tight fingers and burying her face in my shoulder before I bring my lips to her ear and whisper, "Beg me, Caitlin. Tell me not to stop."

"Don't stop," she pants, a quiver in her voice that betrays how close she is to the edge.

I push harder, deeper, making sure she's seconds from shattering when I still my hand and say—

"Beg me."

"God, Gabe," she sobs, her fingers digging into my biceps hard enough to make me wince. "Please."

"More begging," I say, smiling against her skin before I kiss her cheek, her throat, the delicious curve where her neck becomes her shoulder and the smell of her is the strongest. "Beg me like you mean it."

"Fuck you," she growls even as she squirms against my hand, struggling to bring her clit back into contact with my hand.

"If that's what you want," I say. "If you're too proud to beg, then feel free to come on over and you can ride me until—"

She fists her hands in my shirt, shoving me away

for a heartbeat before pulling me in for a bruising kiss. A kiss that steals my focus and threatens to erode my control. After a minute, it's all I can do to keep my hand still inside her, but after several long, breathless minutes with nothing but the sound of our lips and teeth and tongue wrestling in the dark, my patience is rewarded.

"Please touch me," she begs when we come up for air. "Please touch me and keep touching me, please make me come because I want your hand moving inside me so much it's terrifying." She pulls in a breath and lets it out with a sob. "Crazy terrifying, but I want it. I want it so bad."

"Don't be afraid." I resume my thrusts in and out of her adorable pussy, a pussy I'm tempted to christen my favorite without even having tasted it— a first for me. "You can trust me. I would never hurt you. I just want to make you feel good."

"This is so much better than good," she says, words ending in a gasp as I begin to circle my hand, grinding my palm into her clit seconds before my fingers thrust inside her, circling again and again, until she throws back her head, arches her spine, and comes with a cry that is wild and sweet and so perfect I wish I could add it to my favorite playlist and listen to it on endless repeat.

It is perfect, she is perfect, so perfect I don't even notice the police sirens until the patrol car goes rushing past, wailing like a hungry baby.

"Shit," Caitlin says, laughing as she tugs at my wrist. "The police just drove by!"

"The key words being 'drove by.'" I tease my fingers in and out of her one last time before reluctantly giving in to her tugging, and withdrawing my hand from her drenched panties. "They probably didn't even see the car. The shadows are dark."

"What if they had seen us?" Caitlin asks, a challenge in her voice. "What would you have done?"

"Pretended to hold you hostage," I say, hooking my arm around her neck and pulling her close. "Convinced them you were an unwilling victim before turning myself in."

She narrows her eyes. "You're full of it."

"I'm not," I say, before I grin. "At least not about that."

She opens her mouth to say something, but I kiss her before the words can form.

I kiss her with all my hunger for more of her, kiss her with a thoroughness that promises this is a beginning, not an end. I kiss her with the truth of how much I want her, how much she fascinates me, at the front of my mind, hoping that truth will be enough to make up for the lies I've told.

The lies I'll continue to tell, until the day I tell her goodbye.

CHAPTER 9

CAITLIN

Tis sweet to drink, but bitter to pay for. –Irish proverb

One moment really *can* change your life.

One moment, one kiss, one wild night when you color outside the lines, step outside the box, stop playing by the rules….

Gabe and I only spent a few hours together, but now everything is different. Now, the day-to-day grind that was grueling, but survivable—even fun at times—threatens to break me. Now, facts of life I took for granted seem ridiculously unfair. Now, I know how easy it is to turn the tables, and *take* what the world refuses to give people like me.

A chance. A shot at something more if I work hard and give it everything I've got—that's all I want. But it's something I may never have if things don't change.

If I don't *make* them change.

At six in the morning, lying on my lumpy second-hand mattress with the threadbare tee shirt I slept in sticking to my skin in the June heat because there's no way we can run the air conditioning and buy groceries at the same time, with the acid reflux I can't afford to treat burning the back of my throat, it seems like a no brainer. I should call Gabe. I should take him up on his offer to do it all again, to find a new victim, map out another robbery, and take fate into my own hands.

The kids will be out of school in two weeks. After all the snow days in January, classes are running late this year, but come June fifteenth, I'll have three kids in daycare—four if I can convince Terri at the Kiddie Kottage to take Danny, even though he's twelve, and technically too old for daycare.

I can't imagine leaving Danny home alone. He's already getting into trouble. So far he's only been cited for defacing public property—he and the Baker boys down the street decided to spray paint penises on all the neighborhood stop signs, and were dumb enough to get caught. But give my brother a summer to run wild and I have no doubt he'll have more incident reports in his folder down at the police station come August. If I want to keep him out of juvie, I need to make sure Danny has adult supervision while I'm at work.

But adult supervision costs a pretty penny, almost more than I can afford, even with a full time waitressing job, a part time gig selling popcorn at the movie theater, and a subsidy from the state. After paying for daycare last summer, I took home less than four hundred dollars a week. That's sixteen hundred dollars a month to feed, clothe, and shelter a family of five—six if you count my father.

Since he's been shacking up with Veronica, Chuck doesn't *technically* live at the house anymore, but he still sleeps here sometimes—when he's too drunk to remember that he moved into Veronica's apartment above the Laundromat, or when Veronica sobers up enough to realize she's sleeping with a man who regularly forgets to brush his teeth, and kicks Chuck out for a few days.

And when he sleeps here, Chuck eats here and makes messes here and inevitably ends up costing me far more money than he donates to the family coffers. He hasn't had a job in almost a year and drinks away every dime of his VA pension and disability.

So...six people. Six people on sixteen hundred a month.

It's no wonder I almost lost the house in April. If I hadn't robbed the pawnshop, my three brothers and two-year-old niece, Emmie, would be in foster care, and I would be homeless. Homeless, after working my ass off to raise four kids by myself for two-and-a-half years. After dropping out of school, giving up my academic scholarship to Cristoph Prep, and putting every dream I had on the shelf, I would have lost everything. I would have lost my family, the only thing that makes all the back-breaking work worth it.

The property taxes have been paid and that danger has passed for another year, but we're not out of the woods. It will be a struggle to get through the summer, a struggle that will continue into the fall when tourism to historic downtown Giffney slacks off and my tips take a dive. A struggle that will intensify come winter when I'm forced to run the heat in our drafty old house and the electric bill skyrockets.

Gabe was right. There are only two ways out: either let the state take the kids and start looking out for number one—something I could never do, even if I wanted to, even if Emmie, Sean, Ray, and even Danny, that pain in my ass, didn't mean the world to me—or stop playing by the rules.

"And eventually get caught and go to jail," I say to the water-stain on the ceiling, the one I haven't gotten around to painting over since the roof leaked in November. "And have to live with knowing I'm an awful person, and a horrible example to the kids."

But the words don't sound sincere, even to my own ears.

The man we robbed in April was a monster, a miserable excuse for a human being who beat his wife nearly to death, on multiple occasions. He deserved what he got, and Gabe promised me there were others like him, other awful, evil people he'd learned about while trolling through his defense attorney father's files.

I could help make sure creeps who have gotten off scot-free for their crimes are punished. I would be like an instrument of karma, avenging the innocent while lightening my own load in the process.

And if I saved up enough money, I could take time off from work to study and get my GED. It wouldn't take long. Then I'd be able to take classes at the community college, and get qualified for a job that pays better than minimum wage. I'd have more time to spend with the kids on their homework, time to work with Emmie on the speech therapy stuff her therapist said we need to hit harder at home, maybe even time to go out dancing more than once or twice a year.

Dancing…with Gabe.

My lids slide closed and I shiver despite the heat that's making my tee shirt stick to my skin and beads of sweat pool between my breasts.

Visions of that night—my twentieth birthday, the night everything changed—play out in the darkness behind my eyes: Gabe's big hands pulling me into his arms, his fingers digging into my hips, his ice-blue eyes holding me captive in that moment before we kissed, promising wicked, wonderful things as his hand slipped between my legs and he made me shatter into a million beautiful pieces.

But not before he made you beg for it, made you beg him to make you come like some bimbo in a porno.

I open my eyes with a sigh, ignoring the way my

body is tingling simply from thinking about Gabe's touch.

I *did* beg. I begged him to bring me over, and even worse I'd sort of…liked it. *Loved it.* I loved it so much even the memory is enough to make my panties damp, my breasts ache, and my heart beat faster with wanting more. More of Gabe, more of his kiss, his touch, of the rush I felt in his arms.

I don't know how much of that rush was because we'd barely escaped getting shot by the other people breaking into the store, and how much was Gabe—it had all been too tangled up together—but I know the feeling was dangerous.

It was the kind of feeling that made my mother run away with her AA sponsor, never to be heard from again. The kind of feeling that made my big sister bail on her two-month-old daughter, and take off to Columbia with her new, drug-dealer boyfriend.

It was the kind of feeling that could destroy what's left of this family.

Chuck won't even look for a job, let alone take on the responsibility of running a household and raising four kids. If I'm not here for my brothers and Emmie, no one will be. They'll go into the system and be placed in foster homes, homes that could be even worse than the placements I endured when I was younger.

Lice infestations, shaved heads, older foster kids who pinch and hit, foster parents who spend your lunch money on cigarettes, and biological kids who are given your share of supper are shitty things, but there are worse ones. Far worse, and I refuse to be responsible for any of my kids suffering like that.

And, in the end, that's why I haven't picked up the phone. That's why I've ignored the text Gabe sent a week ago saying he had a con job on deck he thought I'd enjoy. That's why I pretend it's only the June heat that has me waking up multiple times a night, drenched in sweat, with my belly aching and my thighs shifting back and forth in an effort to banish the need that's driving me crazy.

I can't give that need an inch, or I'm afraid it will take a mile, take everything I've worked and sacrificed for and leave me hating myself for turning out like my worthless mom and sister. I'm a strong person, but I'm not sure I'm strong enough to survive Gorgeous Gabe Alexander and come out whole on the other side.

"So forget him, forget that night, and get over yourself," I say, with a vicious kick to the thin sheet covering my legs.

But some things are easier said than done.

CHAPTER 10

CAITLIN

Thoughts of Gabe linger in my mind as I hustle down the stairs to the kitchen and shove frozen waffles into the toaster, teasing through my thoughts as I slap peanut butter on bread, drop apples and juice boxes into Ray and Sean's lunch boxes, and use the last of the ham to make Danny a double-decker ham and cheese so he'll have energy for softball practice. Visions of Gabe's stupid-beautiful face flash on my mental screen as I pound back up the stairs, shouting for Sean and Ray to wake up before easing into Danny and Emmie's room, and tiptoeing over to Emmie's toddler bed.

It's only then, when she looks up at me with her big blue eyes and smiles her sweet smile that my head snaps back on straight.

"Good morning, doodle." I gather her into my arms, kissing the warm curve of her neck beneath her blond curls, that place that is still kitten soft and smells like the baby she once was instead of the busy toddler she's becoming.

This sweet little girl is worth the hard work. She's worth living right and staying away from boys like Gabe, and all the trouble that would accompany him and his easy answers.

There are no easy answers, and nothing comes for free. If I let my morals get any more twisted up than they are already, I'll pay for it, one way or another.

"I have a note," Danny says from his bed behind me, his voice thick with sleep.

"What kind of note?" I kiss Emmie's cheek and lean down to fetch her Happy—her name for her pink-and-white-striped blanket—from her nest of covers. She clutches it in her chubby hands and presses it to her face with a content sigh, making me smile.

"From Mr. Pitt. It's in my backpack."

My smile vanishes. "Why didn't you give it to me first thing after softball yesterday?"

"I forgot," Danny says with a grunt, followed by a heavy thud as he jumps from the top of his lofted bed

"Don't jump out of bed," I snap as I turn, hitching Emmie higher on my hip. "You're going to fall through the floor. What's the note about?"

"Special conference." Danny grabs the jeans he wore yesterday from the back of his desk chair and shoves one of his skinny legs inside.

He's shooting up so fast he can't keep on weight.

By the end of the summer, he'll be taller than I am. I'm only five foot one, so that's not saying a lot, but still…I can't believe my brother's getting so big. It scares me a little. He's only twelve, but he's growing up so fast. Soon, he'll be too old to care what his nagging older sister has to say, and way too big for me to have any hope of making him listen.

Danny stretches, his ribs showing through his skin as he pulls a tee shirt from the pile on the floor and sniffs the pits before tugging it over his head. "I think he wants to talk to you after school."

"Crap, when?" I shove my tangled hair off my forehead. "Not today, I hope. I don't get off work until four and I have to be back at the theater by—"

"I don't know! God, just read the note," Danny snaps before vanishing into the hall, headed toward the bathroom.

"Tone, Danny!" I call out after him before turning back to Emmie with a sigh. "Your uncle is a pain in my butt."

"In da butt," Emmie repeats with a grin.

"Yes," I say with a serious nod. "Like a fart."

Emmie's grin becomes a giggle. She doesn't talk as much as the doctors would like a nearly three-year-old to talk, but she loves fart jokes, and I'm not above potty humor in the name of making her dimples pop.

"You ready for breakfast?" I ask, pressing a kiss to her forehead.

She nods, and we head down the stairs to the

ground floor bathroom so the boys can have the one upstairs.

The rest of the morning passes in the usual state of barely controlled chaos. Ray drops the book for his book report in the toilet and I end up blow-drying it with one hand while putting on my make-up with the other. Emmie spills her orange juice on my last clean pair of uniform shorts and I have to dash back upstairs to change into the hideous dress with the puffed sleeves I try not to wear on Fridays because that's the day Mr. Noel comes in for pancakes and his hand has a habit of drifting.

Sean realizes he forgot to do his spelling pre-test and Danny has to give it to him as I'm changing Emmie out of her orange-juice-soaked sleeper and giving her a quick wipe down at the sink. No sooner do I have her clean and dressed for daycare than Ray manages to break the zipper on his backpack and Sean bursts into tears because he got two words wrong on his pre-test and Danny is giving him shit about it.

When I finally herd the savages out the door at ten 'til eight, I'm already exhausted and not looking forward to a six hour shift at the restaurant, followed by another five hour shift at Cinema Eight later tonight.

By the time I've dropped Sean and Ray at the elementary school, deposited Danny at the junior high with a strong warning to stay out of trouble and a note for Mr. Pitt saying I'll have to push this afternoon's conference to Monday, and sprinted Emmie to the front door of the Kiddie Kottage—hopefully giving myself just enough time to grab a coffee at work before I have to clock in—my mind is already drifting back to that easy way out.

As I maneuver the ancient family van through downtown Giffney, it dangles in my thoughts like forbidden fruit, so sweet and juicy I don't see how I'm going to resist taking a bite. I'm hungry for it, starving, so ready for a taste of that easier life it promises, I can practically feel it exploding on my tongue.

And then I see *him*, Gorgeous Gabe, leaning against the weathered bricks of Harry's Diner, his jagged brown hair hanging low over one side of his forehead, looking so delicious in wrinkled black jeans and a whisper-thin gray tee shirt it should be illegal. The moment our eyes meet, his full lips draw into a grin that promises the best kind of trouble, and something breaks inside me.

Inside, I'm already falling, tumbling into the waiting arms of temptation with a sigh of pleasure, standing on tiptoe to claim his lips and taste his wicked taste and tell him how much I've missed the way his eyes light up when he's thinking naughty things about me.

My outsides, however, are a different story.

On the outside, I am calm, cool, collected, and not the least bit interested in what Gabe has to offer. As long as I can hold that facade together, I'll be all right.

"Keep telling yourself that," I mutter as I slam the door to the van shut behind me and start across the street.

Gabe's icy blue eyes drift up and down, taking in my uniform with obvious amusement. "Nice dress."

"What do you want?" I ask in a flat tone, crossing my arms beneath my breasts only to uncross them a second later when I remember how low cut the stupid ruffled collar is. "I only have a second, or I'll be late for work."

Gabe's smile doesn't falter. "I've missed you too, sweetheart."

"I'm not your sweetheart," I say, but I can feel the blush spreading across my cheeks.

A part of me would like to be his sweetheart, to be Gabe's girl, and, more importantly, his partner in crime.

"But you could be." He pushes away from the wall, closing the distance between us, not stopping until he's so close I can smell his soap and trouble smell, the one that makes my mouth water and my skin feel too small. "What do you say? Up for another job? This one needs a feminine touch."

I shake my head as I back away, my pulse leaping at my throat. "No," I say, even as my heart screams *yes* and my fingertips begin to tingle, remembering the rush of plucking a thousand dollars in jewelry from the pawnshop's glass case.

"You don't mean that." He falls in beside me as I start toward the diner's front door. "Come on, Caitlin. Come play with me."

Play. That's all this is to him, some stupid game to help pass the time this summer while he's home from college and working part time at his dad's law firm. Gabe's dad is a successful lawyer, his mom is a high-priced interior decorator, and his grandmother is descended from the town founders, and richer than God. Gabe told me he could buy and sell my entire family at least twice, and I believe him. He isn't desperate the way I am; he's simply bored.

I can't remember the last time I was bored. I'm too exhausted and overworked and stressed out to be bored. Boredom sounds like fucking heaven to me, and the fact that the boy breezing into the coffee shop beside me doesn't realize how lucky he is to have the luxury of boredom pisses me off, and gives me the strength to turn to him and say—

"I'm not your toy, and I don't have time to play." I lower my voice, not wanting my boss, Gretchen, to hear me sassing a customer. "So leave. Now. And don't bother me at work again."

I spin on my heel and flee through the long, narrow aisle of the restaurant, shoving through the swinging doors leading to the kitchen and the tiny staff break room without a backward glance. But I can feel Gabe watching me, the weight of his gaze making me feel heavier and lighter at the same time, making my blood rush and my stomach drop and my traitorous feet want to reverse course and hurry back to his side.

I'm not finished with Gabe; deep down, I know that.

But sometimes success is simply a matter of putting off disaster for one moment and then another and another, keeping the balls in the air for as long as possible before they all come crashing down.

CHAPTER 11

GABE

The lady doth protest too much. –Shakespeare

If I were a nice guy, I would take Caitlin at her word and leave her alone.

But I'm not a nice guy, and I saw the way her eyes lit up when I mentioned the job. She's hooked, just like me. She's had a taste, and she's dying for more. All it will take is a few more nudges and she'll tumble over the edge of hesitation into my arms, where I'll be waiting to catch her.

Catch her, and lead her further along the road we started down two months ago.

Ever since that night in her friend's car, I haven't been able to get Caitlin out of my head. I keep hearing her laugh and those sexy moans she made when I slipped my fingers between her legs, remembering the way her pale throat glowed in the flashing red and blue police lights as she threw her head back and came on my hand. I taste her kiss when I wake up in the night, sweating despite the air conditioning my mother keeps set at sixty-five degrees. I see Caitlin's old-before-her-time green eyes floating in the darkness while I'm lying awake in bed, trying not to think about the future.

I've never been the kind of person to give up on something I want, even back in high school, when I was still resigned to the path my parents had laid out for my life.

Now, I flat out refuse to take no for an answer.

Caitlin is going to agree to this job, and then the next, and the next. We're going to have a summer neither of us will ever forget, and do the world some good while we're at it. And by the time we go our separate ways, she'll have enough money to go to college and stop wasting her life, and I will have had her, every way I want her.

I ease into a booth on the far side of the restaurant and take the sticky menu the older waitress with the gray-streaked brown bun offers. She's wearing the same dress as Caitlin—a short number with a black skirt, red suspenders, and a frilly white apron, apparently inspired by a Bavarian brew house—but the effect is…decidedly different. On the senior waitress, the dress is as tired and out-of-place as the faded, yellowing posters of rural Germany hanging on the walls of this South Carolina diner.

But on Caitlin …

When she pushes back through the double doors, every male head in the restaurant swivels her way. The low cut neck of the dress shows off her curves, while the red band around the middle highlights her tiny waist. Her caramel-streaked honey blonde hair is pulled into a ponytail that emphasizes the graceful column of her neck, and when she walks, her skirt swishes temptingly around her thighs.

That swish makes it impossible to keep my thoughts from drifting back to that night in the VW bug, when she spread her thighs in silent invitation, daring me to find out if breaking and entering had left her as turned on as I was. It had, of course, left her so hot and slick it had only taken me a few minutes to get her off. Just thinking about it is enough to make my jeans tighter, and my hands ache to be sliding up her thighs to cup her ass in my hands.

I want this girl. I want to help her, and fuck her, and steal things with her, and make her laugh the way she did right before we kissed goodbye back in April. I want more time with Caitlin more than I've wanted anything in months, and that alone is reason enough to keep my seat, even when she turns and scowls at me. Not many things hold my interest for more than a few hours at a time these days, but Caitlin Cooney, with her wild streak running through her pathetically responsible, dreary life like a caramel swirl through ice cream just…does it for me.

I watch her cross the restaurant, not phased by the thinning of her lips, or the pinched look on her face. She can put an end to her frustration any time she wants. All she has to do is quit fighting, and give in to what we obviously both want.

"What will you have?" she asks, pen clenched tightly between her fingers, gaze glued to the pad in her hand.

"You, tomorrow night," I say. "At my house, for dinner with my parents. Nothing else, just dinner, conversation, and I'll take you home straight after."

Her eyes flick to mine, surprise clear in their depths. "I thought you said..." She casts a glance over her shoulder at the older waitress wiping down the stainless steel counter before turning back to me and continuing in a whisper, "I thought you said it was a job."

"It is. A con job," I say. "I'll pay you five hundred dollars to pretend to be my girlfriend for the night."

"Five hundred..." A smile teases at the edge of her lips. "You're kidding."

"I'm not. Five hundred dollars for one night of pretend."

She narrows her eyes, obviously looking for the catch. "Why? Why do you need a pretend girlfriend?"

"My mother insists on setting me up with girls she meets through her volunteer work. She thinks I need a girlfriend to turn my life around." That's not exactly why my mother is so determined to see me in love, but it's close enough. "She refuses to let it go, no matter how many times I insult the nice young women she dumps in my lap. A fake summer love is the only way I can think of to get her to leave me alone."

Caitlin points the business end of her pen at my face. "I thought you said it was only for the night."

"Five hundred dollars for the night, with an option to rebook if my mother requires further conning," I clarify. "Future dates and payments to be negotiated on a case by case basis."

Caitlin casts another glance over her shoulder. This time, the older waitress is watching her with a sour expression.

"Just order something," Caitlin whispers as she turns back to me. "Or I'm going to get into trouble."

"Two eggs—scrambled—toast, and your answer," I say. "I'll take it all to go."

She rolls her eyes before bringing pen to pad, muttering beneath her breath, "At least it's not illegal."

"Not at all."

"I wasn't talking to you," she says with a glare that is more cute than menacing. "Your total is eight seventy-six. Have the money ready when I get back. I want you out of here."

"Why?" I ask, lifting a wry brow. "Am I distracting you?"

"You're annoying me," she says, but she doesn't sound annoyed. She sounds intrigued, and I know she's going to give in even before she returns with my breakfast in a brown paper bag and plops it down in front of me with a curt nod.

"I'll do it." She holds up a finger, stopping me before I can respond. "But I want payment up front, in cash. I'll have to take off work at the theater tomorrow night, and I can't afford to do that unless I'm sure I'm getting paid. And I go straight home after. No…other stuff. Strictly business."

"You're blushing," I say, loving the fact that she's flustered by our relatively tame history. But maybe she's never begged a guy to make her come before. I hope not. I wouldn't mind being the first man to show Caitlin how fun playing dirty can be.

"I'm not blushing." She rolls her eyes again, and her cheeks grow pinker. "Agree to my terms, or it's a no go. I told you, I don't have time to play."

But you will, if I have anything to say about it.

Aloud I say, "It's a deal. I'll pick you up at six."

"Fine." She tears the ticket off her pad and drops it on the table beside the bag. "But don't come to the door. I'll meet you in the driveway. I don't want to have to explain you to the kids."

"They don't usually meet your dates?"

"I don't date," she says as I pull my wallet from my jeans pocket. "I don't have time, and I don't plan on making any, so don't get any ideas."

I drop a twenty on top of the check. "I've never had an idea in my life."

Her lips quirk, but she doesn't allow the twitch to become a smile. "Yeah, right. You're full of ideas.

All of them bad, as far as I can tell. You know your parents are going to hate me, right?"

"Why's that?" I ask, though I know exactly why, and know she would have been right, even a few months ago.

"I'm a high school dropout who works as a waitress," she says in a matter of fact tone, obviously not ashamed of who she is, "with a father who's been arrested for drunk and disorderly more times than I can count. Your parents will probably be scared to death you'll get me pregnant, and they'll be permanently tied to the tackiest family in Giffney."

"How can I get you pregnant if there's no 'other stuff' allowed?"

She swipes the twenty and the check from the table and mumbles, "Your parents won't know that."

"I could tell them," I say, not wanting her to go. "I could tell them you're a virgin who's saving herself for marriage. My mom would love that, even if she is already talking grandchildren."

"Tell them whatever you want," Caitlin says in a chilly voice. "As long as you're paying me, I don't care."

"Maybe I will." I smile, some perverse part of me enjoying pissing her off.

"Fine," she snaps. "I'll be right back with your change."

She spins so fast her skirt swirls higher on her legs, making the old man settling into the booth across from mine inhale sharply and his eyes bulge in his red face. I watch her hips twitch as she storms across the restaurant and behind the counter to the register, knowing I should feel guilty for making her angry. But she's even prettier when she's angry, with her cheeks all red and those green eyes flashing.

Besides, I'll make up for being an asshole later, when I treat her like a princess all evening and my mother spends the entire dinner falling all over herself to welcome Caitlin to the family. There was a time when my mother wanted only the best for me—which, in her mind, included a girlfriend with money, ambition, and the proper pedigree—but now she just wants to see me in love, to see me so gone on a girl I'll have a reason to fight to reverse my life's sudden downward trajectory.

My mother still believes in happy endings. She thinks I'll convince the university that those failing grades and missed classes back in March were excusable lapses in judgment, and they'll welcome me back to school in the fall with open arms. She talks about the grandchildren I'll bring home to Darby Hill for long visits in the summer, despite the fact that all signs—and my failure to commit to any of the girls I've casually dated—point to grandchildren as being the stuff of fantasy.

My mother's more likely to find a unicorn frolicking in the back forty than a kid in my future, but there's no reasoning with Deborah once she's got her mind set on something.

That's why I need Caitlin. I could have found another girl to pretend with me, but I wouldn't have been able to trust her the way I trust Caitlin. We committed a felony together. After that, deceiving my parents will be a walk in the park. I know I can trust her not to mention any of the forbidden topics I'll list on the way to dinner, to stay on task, and to keep her emotional distance and not be drawn in by my mother's attempts to worm her way deeper into my girlfriend's life.

I'm truly looking forward to getting on with my summer agenda without any blind dates on the horizon, but having an excuse to spend time with Caitlin is an excellent bonus.

"I'm ready to order, sugar," the old man in the booth across from mine says in a syrupy voice as Caitlin hustles back to our corner of the restaurant.

"I'll be right with you, Mr. Noel. Just one second." She turns to me, and starts counting out my change, but I'm still looking at Mr. Noel, who is looking at Caitlin's ass in a way no man old enough to be her grandfather should be looking at her ass.

Hell, in a way *no* other man should *ever* be allowed to look at her ass. Caitlin may not be mine, yet, but she will be, and the unapologetic lust in the geezer's faded blue eyes is enough to make my blood boil.

"Hey, friend," I say, venom in my tone. "Keep your eyes where they belong."

The old man blinks, his gaze drifting from Caitlin's ass, to me, to Caitlin's ass, and back again before he seems to realize the words were meant for him. "Excuse me?"

"Keep your eyes on her face, or you'll regret it." I slide out of the booth and stand, staring down at him with a hard look I hope makes it clear this isn't an idle threat. "She deserves your respect, and her ass isn't on the menu."

"Gabe stop," Caitlin hisses behind me. She grabs my elbow and slips around my left side, inserting herself between me, and the creep scooting to the edge of his booth. "I'm so sorry, Mr. Noel. My friend is crazy, he—"

"I'm not crazy. Mr. Noel knows he was out of line."

"I'll get pancakes somewhere else," the man mumbles, his eyes on the ground and his spotted hand clutching his chest as he shuffles toward the door.

"Good idea." I watch him go, half hoping the pervert has a heart attack on the way out. He's already had more than his fair share of time on Earth, and his death would mean one fewer slime ball oozing around the planet.

But it seems like the worst people are the ones who stick around the longest. The files in my father's office are full of old men and women who have lived long, shitty lives.

They say only the good die young.

I'm not sure that's true, but the evil certainly seem to linger.

The old man is nearly to the door when the other waitress rushes over, laying a hand on his back as she leans in to ask him if he's okay.

"I'm fine, Gretchen, sugar." His anxious eyes shift my way. "Just know when I'm not wanted."

"What?" Gretchen turns, pinning me with an outraged look before her eyes slide to Caitlin and freeze over. "Caitlin, come apologize to Mr. Noel. Right now."

I snag Caitlin's elbow as she starts forward. "*He* should be the one apologizing."

"Let me go." Caitlin tugs her arm away and points to the exit, adding beneath her breath, "Just leave. Please. You've caused enough trouble for one morning."

"I'm trying to help." I snatch the bag containing my breakfast from the table. "You're better than this. You should quit."

"Leave," she repeats, putting a hand between my shoulder blades, urging me toward the exit with more strength than I expected. "This isn't helping. Not even a little bit."

"All right, if you won't listen to reason…" I amble to the front of the restaurant, holding the older waitress's cool gaze as I move, making it clear I'm not sorry for calling out the pervert she has tucked protectively under her arm.

Gretchen gives as good a glare as she gets, but Mr. Noel seems determined to keep his focus on the ground until I'm gone, so I'm forced to settle for a whispered—

"Remember what we talked about."

—as I slip out the door, instead of the moment of eye contact I would have preferred.

LILI VALENTE

As soon as the door shuts behind me, I hear the older waitress snap at Caitlin, followed by the enraging sound of Caitlin apologizing. I want to turn around and kick Mr. Noel to the curb myself, but instead, I cross the small parking lot. I lift my face to the morning sun already glaring down from the sky, not allowing my eyes to drift toward the restaurant until I reach the Beamer.

When I do glance back, I wish I hadn't. I could have done without seeing Caitlin with her head bowed and her spine curved submissively before Mr. Noel, like a dog with its tail tucked between its legs. She isn't the strong, wild, fearless girl who climbed over a barbed wire fence with me now. She looks beaten, tired, and so much older than twenty.

Seeing her like this—so small and unable to fight back, at the mercy of the people she depends upon for this shit job—stirs up unexpected feelings. I suddenly want to take Caitlin away from this place, to hold her hand as I walk her to my car and apologize for making her life more difficult. I want to do something to make up for the crap people in the world, and be a better friend to her than I was this morning.

The past few months, I've done my best to dispose of my old friends. I don't need to make any new ones, especially not a friend who dances like there's no one watching, has a smile that makes me want to learn all her secrets, and kisses like the world is on fire.

Caitlin Cooney is dangerous, and starting to

look less like the answer to my problems, and more like trouble I don't need.

I should put an end to this thing between us before it begins. I should put the money I promised her in an envelope and stick it in her mailbox, with a note telling her I've changed my mind about dinner. I should delete her number from my phone, and forget I know where she lives. I should walk away from Caitlin Cooney and stay the hell out of her life.

But I won't.

I've never been good at doing what I should. I don't resist Temptation, I throw him a big, loud party and invite Trouble to D.J.

CHAPTER 12

CAITLIN

Even a small thorn causes festering. –Irish Proverb

Saturday night, I pace the length of the living room for the fifth time in less than ten minutes. I swipe the dusty blue curtains to one side, peeking at the empty driveway.

Gabe will be here any minute. Any freaking minute.

Why did I say yes to this? Why did I agree to this stupid, stress-inducing, fake date?

"Won't he honk?" Heather, my best friend Isaac's girlfriend, asks.

"He'd better not." Isaac glances up from the bloody Xbox game he and Danny are playing while the little kids play outside. He sits up straighter on the couch, puffing out his broad chest. "He'd better come to the door and let me glare at him so he knows to behave himself."

Heather laughs, twirling one of her tight brown curls around her finger as she keeps an eye on the pasta boiling on the stove. "You're not Caitlin's dad, Isaac."

"Thank God," I mumble, glancing toward the back door, half expecting Chuck to stumble in drunk off his ass and ruin this date before it starts.

I trust Isaac and Heather to watch the kids, but I don't trust anyone to handle Chuck, but me. My dad has been known to get belligerent with non-family members—and occasionally gets rough with Danny if my brother insists on running his mouth—but my father has never raised a hand to me, not once in my entire life. I can always get him talked down from the edge and tucked safely into bed.

Chuck has ruined my plans many, *many* times before—he has a sixth sense that alerts him on the rare occasions when I've arranged to do something fun—but this time around a Chuck crisis might be a blessing in disguise.

I have no idea what I'm going to say to Gabe's parents, or how I'm going to convince them that Gabe and I are in love. I barely know the guy, and considering how much trouble he caused at the diner yesterday, I'm feeling more inclined to punch him in the gut than hold his hand at the supper table.

Liar. Such a terrible liar.

I sigh, and busy myself laying out plates and

silverware for the pasta dinner Heather graciously offered to cook.

I *am* a terrible liar. Hearing someone call out Mr. Noel before he could get a hand up my skirt was one of the highlights of my year, and totally worth incurring Gretchen's wrath. Gretchen is always miffed with someone. By Monday, she'll be pissed at one of the other servers and forget she threatened to fire me, but Mr. Noel won't be putting his hands on me again. And I have Gabe to thank for it.

Gabe, who sounded like he actually cared whether I was treated well at work, who sounded like he cared about *me*…

"But he doesn't," I mutter, tossing the final fork onto a napkin and heading back into the kitchen. "He's a huge, asshole player."

"Then why are you going out with him?" Isaac asks.

"Talking to myself," I call out, snagging the salad I made earlier from the fridge.

"I don't care," Isaac says. "I heard it, and I want to know why you're breaking your 'no dating ever' rule for some guy you don't even like."

"She didn't say she didn't like him," Heather says, eyes dancing in her pale face.

She's given up the Goth makeup she loved senior year of high school, but with her ivory skin, dark eyes, and thick brown curls, she still looks like the heroine of a vampire novel. She and Isaac, who is about as gothic looking as a cocker spaniel, are a mismatched couple looks-wise, but their personalities fit just right. They're one of the most functional couples I've ever met, and I love having them around. It's good for the kids—hell, for me—to see a romantic relationship can actually work.

"She said he was an asshole player," Heather continues, a teasing note in her voice. "You can still like a player. I mean, I have dirty dreams about Howie all the time, and he treated me like crap when we were dating and broke up with me on my birthday."

"Hey, I heard that." Isaac glares across the room, making Heather laugh. "Seriously babe, I didn't want to hear that."

Heather shrugs. "I'm just saying, sometimes a girl can't help falling for the wrong guy."

"I'm not falling for him." I plunk the salad down on the table, barely resisting the urge to go peek out the window again. "I'm doing him a favor. His parents want him to have a girlfriend, so I'm pretending to be his girlfriend. It's like...a job."

"Why do his parents care if he has a girlfriend?" Danny asks, his disdain for this "date night" obvious in his tone.

"Some parents actually care if their kids are going to get married and have a family someday," Isaac says, the fact that he has to explain that to my brother making my chest feel bruised. "It's a real thing."

"I want you to get married and have a family someday too, D," I say. "Someday far, far from now when you're at least twenty-three and have a really good job."

Danny snorts. "I'm not getting married."

"You'll change your mind," Isaac says. "You'll start liking girls sooner than you think."

"I like girls fine." Danny blows up a zombie's head, filling the television screen with blood splatter. "I just don't want to get tied down. I'm going to be an asshole player. Like Caitlin's date."

"You see this? This is what comes of talking grown up stuff in front of the children." I step over to the couch and knuckle Danny's head.

"Ow!" Danny smacks my hand away without taking his attention from the screen. "You're not a grownup. You can't even get into a club without a fake I.D."

Before I can ask Danny how he knows about my fake I.D.—or check to make sure the I.D. is still in my purse, and my brother hasn't "liberated" it the way he liberated the fireworks I hid in my closet last summer, or the six pack of Coke I tucked behind the bill box on top of the refrigerator in hopes of keeping a can for myself for once—there's a knock on the front door.

My stomach flips and acid burns the back of my throat. I'm considering grabbing a roll of Tums before hurrying to the door to whisk Gabe away before anyone can meet him, when the door swings open, revealing a very dressed up Gabe. He's wearing an expensive looking suit, and holding a red-faced, hiccupping Emmie in his arms. Sean and

Ray are not far behind them, pounding up the stairs and into the house seconds after Gabe steps inside.

"What happened?" I hustle across the room, irritation that Gabe didn't stay in the driveway forgotten in my hurry to get to Emmie.

"Sean let Emmie get on his old bike, even though I told him not to," Ray said, words emerging in a breathless rush as I reach for Emmie and she dives into my arms.

I run my fingers gently over her face, wiping her sweat-damp curls off her forehead as my eyes skim the rest of her, finding no obvious injuries aside from a bloody knee and a scrape on her hand.

"I told him she was still too little," Ray continues, "but he wouldn't listen."

"It has training wheels!" Sean shouts, sounding near tears himself. "It's not my fault she didn't know how to use the brakes."

"It *is* your fault!" Ray shouts back. "I told you, she's just a baby!"

"But you're the oldest, Ray," I say in my "calm down" voice as I start toward the kitchen. "You should have come to get me if Sean wouldn't listen. Now, is it just the scrapes on her hand and knee? Did she hit her head?"

"He's eight, that's old enough to know better," Ray says, ignoring my question. "I don't know why I always get blamed for everything!"

"Ray, come on," I say as he turns and flees up the stairs. "I didn't mean—"

I break off with a sigh and a roll of my eyes,

continuing into the kitchen, knowing there's no point in going after Ray. When Ray's upset, he locks himself in the upstairs bathroom and nothing can coax him out. He'll take a long bath and emerge when he's good and ready, and no amount of sweet-talking on my part will make a damned bit of difference.

"I pulled up right as she fell." Gabe appears beside me as I settle Emmie on the edge of the sink, bracing her back with one of his big hands as I turn on the water, surprising me with how comfortable he seems amidst the chaos. "She caught herself and didn't hit the pavement too hard. I think she's more scared than anything."

"Well, yeah," I say, catching Emmie's eye, glad to see her tears have stopped. "It's scary not to be able to stop. Right, doodle?"

Emmie nods, watching me run cool water over her knee before glancing up at Gabe. She's usually not big on strangers, but he doesn't seem to be freaking her out. I'm sure the fact that he came to her rescue is helping.

"But you were doing great before you fell," Gabe says, using his normal voice, earning instant points for not talking to Emmie like she's a dog, the way a lot of people do when they talk to little kids. "Stopping is easy once you learn how. I bet Caitlin can teach you."

Emmie widens her eyes at me.

"Of course I can," I assure her, answering her unspoken question. "We'll have a lesson tomorrow morning. But with jeans on, so you won't get an owie if you fall."

"Owie," Emmie echoes, squirming her bare toes as I gently pat her knee dry with a paper towel.

"Can you make sure she doesn't fall off the counter while I get medicine and a Band-Aid?" I ask Gabe, flustered by how close he's standing.

Now that the situation with Emmie is under control, I'm realizing how amazing he looks in his dark blue suit with an ice blue tie the same color as his eyes, and how much smaller the kitchen suddenly seems with him in it.

Gabe isn't as big as Isaac—few people are, Isaac is a six-foot-four bear of a person—but for some reason Gabe seems to take up more space. It's something about his posture or the directness of his gaze or...something. I'm not exactly sure what it is, but I know by the time I've crawled up on the counter to fetch a bandage and antibiotic ointment I feel self-conscious, and very aware of the fact that Sean, Isaac, and Heather are standing on the other side of the island, watching as Gabe and I finish up with Emmie.

"There, good as new." I scoop Emmie off the counter, pressing a kiss to her cheek before setting her on the ground and watching her toddle off past Danny, still sprawled on the couch, toward the toy chest in the corner of the living room.

Isaac turned off the bloody videogame once the other kids came inside, and the house is weirdly quiet. So quiet it feels like everyone is listening when I turn to Gabe and ask—

"So, um…should I change, or what?"

He glances down at my pale yellow sundress with the lace accents at the hem. It's one of my favorites, but it feels too casual now that I've seen what "dressed for dinner" means for the Alexander family.

"This is great," he says. "You look beautiful."

"Are you sure? I mean you're so…" I motion up and down, cheeks heating when Gabe smiles in a way that makes it clear he's enjoying seeing me at a loss for words.

"I'm sure," he says.

I huff, blowing a few stray wisps of hair from my face. "Okay, fine. Then let's get out of here."

"Should I be introduced first?" Gabe casts a pointed look toward the other side of the island, where Isaac is hovering, looking mildly threatening. Isaac is a relentlessly cheerful person without a lot of glaring experience. He can only pull off mildly threatening, even when he's trying really hard, but still, a scowl is a scowl.

I shoot him a wide-eyed look, silently begging him to cut it out, but my best friend is apparently serious about standing in for my absent father. His glare stays firmly in place, even when I add a shake of my head to the bug eyes.

"Yeah, we'd like to be introduced," Isaac says, ignoring me.

"Of course," I say through gritted teeth, stomach

burning as I lead the way into the living room. "Gabe, these are my friends, Isaac and Heather, from the neighborhood, who watch the kids for me on Saturday nights. Guys, this is Gabe, an old friend from Christoph Academy."

"Nice to meet you." Heather waves, and Isaac holds out a stiff hand.

Isaac and Gabe shake in a way that is weirdly grown up, and also just weirdly weird, and makes me even more eager to get out of the house. I don't know why Isaac is pulling the protective big brother act—he's the one who's always saying I should go on dates every once and awhile—but it's making me nervous.

Not to mention how plain *wrong* it feels for Gabe to be inside my house.

Gabe isn't a part of my real life. He's an alien from a strange, wild world I visited once in the dark. I never intended to introduce him to my family, and no matter how nice he was to Emmie, or the friendly note in his voice when he asks Isaac how long the two of us have been friends, I wish Gabe had stayed outside. I wish he'd never seen how shabby the inside of our house is, and I'd never seen him holding Emmie like she was something precious he wanted to protect.

"And those two are Sean and Danny," I say, pointing to the couch, where Danny is turning on the T.V. "Danny's the blond one who looks like me."

"Do not. Gag," Danny says, not taking his eyes off the television as he flips through our few channels. "Remind me to dye my hair black tomorrow, Sean."

"The one with curly brown hair is Sean," I say, ignoring Danny. "And the other one with brown hair who disappeared is Ray. And you've met Emmie so…that's it. The entire clan. Ready to go?"

"Whenever you are." Gabe turns back to Isaac and Heather. "Nice to meet you. Thanks for helping me get Caitlin out of the house."

"We're always here for Caitlin," Isaac says in a vaguely ominous tone.

"Good to know." Gabe puts an arm around my waist that makes me flinch with surprise, Isaac scowl, and Heather laugh.

"Down, boy," she says to Isaac, threading an arm through his before she turns back to me with a grin. "Have a great time, and don't worry about the kids. We've got everything under control."

"Thanks so much," I mumble, fleeing toward the door, determined to escape before things get any weirder.

I snag my purse, shout good-bye to the kids, and shoo Gabe out of the house in front of me with an anxious flap of my hands. The moment the door slams behind us—providing a thin barrier between my real life and my Gabe life—I feel a hundred times better.

"Thank God that's over," I say, sighing as I lead the way to the ridiculously expensive car parked in my driveway.

The silver BMW probably cost more than our

house, and is definitely going to be the priciest ride I've ever been inside. Gabe's lucky he didn't get his fancy hubcaps stolen. If it had been later, and a little darker on the street, he wouldn't have escaped our neighborhood unscathed.

"You didn't tell me you had a body guard," Gabe says, reaching down to open the passenger's door for me like this is a real date.

"Isaac isn't usually like that." I glance back over my shoulder at the house before I slide into the supple leather seat. "I don't know what's up with him."

"He's protective. I like it." Gabe slams the door, taking his time walking around the front of the car to the driver's side, giving me another long moment to appreciate how fucking stunning he looks.

Why he's back in Giffney, instead of off frolicking with the rich and famous, is beyond me. If I had the kind of money he has, I'd buy a one-way ticket to anywhere but here. Anywhere but this dead end town with its dead end jobs and my deadbeat dad and all the sad memories and stories that follow my family around, making sure no one ever expects much from a Cooney. If I could pack up the kids and give them a fresh start somewhere new, I would do it in a heartbeat.

"I won't worry about you as much now," Gabe says as he settles into the car, banishing the question on the tip of my tongue.

I was going to ask why he sticks around Giffney if he's so bored it's driving him to a life of crime, but now all I can think about is Gabe worrying about me. Why would he worry about me? We barely know each other, and worry implies a level of concern for my welfare I assumed Gabe didn't possess.

I study him out of the corner of my eye as he starts the car and shifts into reverse, doing my best not to fidget when he puts an arm behind my seat and turns to look through the back glass. His face is so close to mine I can smell the spicy, soapy smell of him, that same scent that lingered on my clothes all the way home after I dropped him at the bus stop the night of our heist. By the time I got home, I'd been half drunk with lust, and wishing I'd had the guts to accept his invitation to meet up after he hid the money and jewelry.

I had never been tempted by that kind of invitation before, but that night...

"What are you thinking?" Gabe brakes in the middle of the street, attention shifting to my face as he puts the car in drive.

"Nothing," I say, voice more breathless than I would like.

"Liar," he says. "Tell me. I dare you."

I lick my lips. "You first."

"I'm thinking that....you have a family worth fighting for," Gabe says, holding my gaze with an intensity that makes me certain he knows all my secrets. "And that the way you love them is special. They're lucky to have you."

I blink, eyes stinging at the unexpected compliment. "Well…thanks. They're everything to me so…"

"And you're everything to them. Don't doubt it. Even the troublemaker adores you," he says with a wink before turning his gaze to the street. "Danny, right?"

I laugh as he pulls out of our cul-de-sac onto Newberry Street. "Yeah, Danny. We butt heads constantly." I cast Gabe an assessing look. "You pegged him pretty fast."

"I'm an excellent judge of character." He reaches over, capturing my hand in his, sending a zinging sensation shooting up my arm.

I curl my fingers around his palm, trying to ignore how intimate it feels to hold hands with Gabe, grateful that he seems to have forgotten that I didn't honor my half of our dare. If I had to tell him I was thinking about how much I wished I'd gone home with him after our last date—if you can call robbing a pawnshop, and making out in my best friend's car, a date—it will be more difficult to ensure this date goes according to plan.

I may have been hired to be a fake girlfriend, but there's nothing fake about the way my body hums with happiness, simply to be sitting next to Gabe. There's nothing fake about the way his touch makes me ache, or the soft, melting feeling in my chest left behind by what he said.

I never imagined Gabe would see the beauty in my fucked up family, or be the type to understand the value of unconditional love. Love like that *is* precious, and absolutely worth fighting for. The fact that he realizes that makes me look at him differently, makes me wonder what else Gabe is hiding beneath the bad boy exterior. I had assumed "what you see is what you get" with him, but maybe I was wrong.

The thought creeps in on spider feet, making me shiver. I can't decide which is more dangerous—the player, or the man with a secret soft side. In my experience, secrets breed secrets, and no one puts as much effort into hiding as Gabe does without a damned good, and often frightening, reason.

CHAPTER 13

GABE

She's beautiful, and therefore to be wooed;
She is woman, and therefore to be won
-Shakespeare

While I drive, Caitlin scans the list of off-limits dinner conversation topics I typed into my phone earlier this afternoon. She mutters beneath her breath, and laughs softly when she reaches the end. "The weather?"

"My mother supports global warming research, but my father doesn't believe in climate change," I say, guiding the Beamer onto the country road leading to Darby Hill, the plantation that's been in my family for generations, wishing Caitlin and I were driving in the opposite direction.

After meeting her family, I'm even less eager to introduce her to mine.

There's a reason my parents only have one child. One was all it took for them to realize parenting wasn't for them. They like me well enough, and my mother took to managing me with the same enthusiasm she devotes to all her pet causes, but I saw more tenderness tonight at Caitlin's house than I've ever seen from my parents.

Growing up, my nanny washed my scraped knees when I fell, and easy family banter and shared jokes were things I watched on television. I was expected to keep quiet at the dinner table until I was old enough to contribute to the conversation in a meaningful way, and neither of my parents spent much time with me until I was in high school. I was sixteen before my parents finally took a vested interest—my father when he learned I seemed to share his love of the law, and my mother when I was old enough for her to play matchmaker and set me up with the daughters of all her snobby friends.

I already knew Caitlin had a softer heart than either of my parents—she wouldn't have sacrificed so much for her brothers and niece if she didn't—but I hadn't been prepared for what I saw tonight.

The love Caitlin feels for her family is bigger than anything I've ever witnessed up close, overflowing in every touch, every kiss, even the way she shouted at one brother and rolled her eyes at the other. It was unexpectedly beautiful, and made her even prettier—something I'd assumed was impossible. Caitlin's outsides are something special, but her heart is...stunning. Even after fifteen minutes of driving, I still feel a little dazed. My throat is tight and my chest aches, but not in a bad way, in a hopeful way, though I don't know what the hell I'm hoping for.

I have no right to be hopeful. Nothing has changed. I still have secrets I'm determined to keep, and Caitlin and I still have an expiration date set in stone.

There is no "You and Caitlin." You're on a fake date, and she's only promised you one night.

It's true, but there was something in the way she held my hand as we pulled away from her house, a tenderness that wasn't there before, that made me think she might be developing a soft spot in that heart of hers.

A soft spot for me…

"Okay, whatever you say, boss." She sighs as she drops my phone into the cup holder on her side of the car. "No talking about weather, money, anyone's health, court cases, *your* college, *my* job, or religion. I think I can remember all that, but… what else is there? What am I supposed to talk about?"

"You can talk about the kids," I say, but immediately rethink it. "Though my mom and dad aren't into children. They prefer people over the age of eighteen."

Caitlin frowns and shifts in her seat to face me. "I thought you said your mom wanted grand-children."

"She does. But she'll enjoy the *idea* of grandchildren more than the actual kids." I shrug. "Not that it matters. I'm not having children."

"Me either," Caitlin says. "The boys and Emmie are plenty for me."

I glance at her, a little surprised. "You don't want to be a mother? Seems like you've got a knack for it."

"Thanks." She shoots me a strange look, but I'm forced to turn my attention back to the curving road before I can decipher it.

"If things were different, I would want kids of my own," she continues. "But I'm tired already. By the time I get Emmie raised, I don't think I'll have any energy left."

"Does that make you sad?"

"A little, maybe, but it doesn't matter," she says. "Things are the way they are. No point crying over something I can't change."

I nod. She's right. Some things are the way they are. There's no changing them, no matter how much you want to, and tears are a waste of time and energy.

Other problems, however, *can* be solved—with money. Money can buy free time, free time can breed opportunity, and opportunities can transform a life, especially for someone as focused and determined as Caitlin. The way I see it, almost all of her troubles could be solved with an injection of money into her life, and I intend to make sure she gets it, one way or another.

"The five hundred dollars is in my wallet," I say,

turning down the smooth, freshly paved drive leading to Darby Hill, a black ribbon that winds through gnarled live oak trees my great grandfather planted nearly two hundred years before. "I'll get it for you before we go in. I meant to give it to you at your place, but I—"

"Don't worry about it," Caitlin says. "I'll get it later. I know you're good for it."

"You trust me, then?" I ask, slowing as we reach the end of the drive.

"I trust you more than I did, even if you did almost cost me my job." Caitlin leans forward, eyes widening as Darby Hill comes into view.

The house dates back to the late 1800's, and was built after the original plantation burned to the ground during the Civil War. It's a colonial revival with creamy, pale brick walls, a burnt orange tiled roof with the three garret windows, and eight pillars crowded around the entryway. In addition to having at least four too many pillars, the house boasts a curved veranda on each side, making it look like it's wearing one of those hip bustles women in Europe wore under their skirts for a time, the ones that made it impossible for them to walk through a door without turning sideways.

It's ridiculous, but stunning in its way. Compared to Caitlin's two-story ranch with the sagging roof and crude, concrete steps standing in for the porch that seems to have been stripped away and never replaced, it's a palace.

A palace I would gladly exchange for a seat at the crowded table in the corner of Caitlin's living room.

Since I dropped out of school in March, I've spent a lot of time thinking about what really matters in life, and a giant house is nowhere on the list. Money is well and good, but after a certain point it's an overload of icing that destroys your ability to appreciate the cake. Darby Hill is a monster built by slaves stolen from their country, and maintained by my father's and grandfather's less than ethical law practice. It should have been donated to the state years ago, but my parents don't see anything wrong with clinging to privilege paid for with blood and pain.

I have more than the average rich boy's disdain for abundance, but I should know better than to assume Caitlin, or anyone else in her position, can walk away from a paying job without making sure she has a safety net in place.

"I'm sorry about yesterday." I pull around the circular drive, parking in my usual spot by the azalea bushes. "I didn't like the way that man was looking at you, but I should have thought about the trouble I might cause before I spoke."

Caitlin's gaze drops to the console between us before she glances back up, a smile teasing the edges of her mouth. "To be honest, I'm glad you said something. Noel's been putting his hand up my skirt for years. Now I'll be able to wear a dress on Fridays without having to watch my back every time I bend over to pick up a plate."

"Let me know if he needs a reminder to behave." The thought of the old fuck's hands anywhere on Caitlin makes me wish it was acceptable to punch senior citizens. "Until I can convince you it's safe to quit, I'm happy to help."

"I'm not—" Caitlin breaks off with a sigh and a shake of her head.

"What?" I ask, in no hurry to get out of the car, though I know my mother is probably waiting by the front door. I'm surprised she isn't out on the veranda, watching the driveway—she was *that* thrilled when I told her I was bringing my girlfriend to dinner.

Caitlin's brow furrows. "Why do you care?"

"You're my partner in crime," I say with a shrug, refusing to think too much about the question, or how much I'm coming to care.

"That was one night."

"There will be more."

"No, there won't," she says. "I'm not going to do anything else illegal, Gabe. If I get caught, it's not just my life I'd ruin. I can't put the kids at risk. There's nobody left to pick up the pieces if I go to jail."

"What if I could promise that you won't get caught?" I reach out, capturing a lock of her silky soft hair and twining it around my finger.

"You can't promise something like that," she says, but she doesn't pull away. She leans in and her lips part, and I know she feels the pull I feel.

It's the lure of the forbidden, the rush that

comes from breaking the rules—not because of any desire to be truly bad, but because the rules are wrong. The rules are lies that deserve to be exposed, shattered, ripped apart and sewn back together in a shape that does the world some good. We could do that, Caitlin and I…do the world a little good, while getting high on breaking the law.

"And you shouldn't make promises you can't keep," she adds, a tremble in her voice.

"I don't." Before she can say another word, I silence her with a kiss.

I don't intend it to be a passionate kiss—we have to go inside soon—but the moment my lips touch Caitlin's the world catches fire all over again. Our second kiss is even hotter than our first. Within seconds I'm drunk on her smell, her taste, deliciously jarred by the electricity that leaps between us like we were made to complete a circuit. My fingers bury themselves in her hair and my tongue slips inside her mouth and every nerve ending in my body ignites.

The sensation starts at the base of my spine and spirals out, waves of heat and longing that course through me, making me press closer, kiss deeper, tangling my tongue with hers. Her fingers come to my face and her nails dig into my jaw and I moan, a sound she echoes, vibrating my lips, a buzzing I feel over every inch of my skin.

By the time I pull away, I'm hard enough to shatter glass and don't know how I'm going to make it through dinner. The only taste I want in my mouth right now is Caitlin's.

"I want to have you for dinner," I say, fingers tightening in her hair.

"We agreed," she says, breath coming faster. "No other stuff."

"*After* we leave my parents' house." I press a kiss to her throat, where her pulse leaps beneath her skin. "We didn't say anything about making out in the guest bathroom."

"Stop it, Gabe."

"That's what you said last time, but if I remember correctly, you didn't *really* want me to stop." I kiss the warm skin beneath her ear as I let my fingers trail down her neck, across her chest, down to cup her breast through her dress, drawing a gasp from her lips as I find her pebbled nipple and roll it between my fingers.

Her fingers dig into my shoulders as her breath rushes back in. "Just when I was starting to think you were a nice guy…"

"Let's get inside; I'll show you how nice I can be." I release her breast with extreme reluctance, the kind that can only be overcome by knowing I'm going to have more of her—all of her—in a few minutes. "We'll go in the back door and sneak up the servant stairs. My parents won't figure out where we are until—"

A door slams, cutting off my words.

Caitlin's eyes fly wide. "Your parents?"

"My mother, I'm guessing."

"Jesus, Gabe!" Caitlin braces her hands on my chest, shoving me back across the car before running a hand through her hair, smoothing her skirt, and wiping the edges of her lips. By the time my mother appears at the passenger's side door, grinning like she's just been awarded the Nobel Peace Prize, Caitlin has pulled herself together and I've thrown a casual arm over my rapidly flagging erection.

Nothing kills a hard on like a guy's mother. Especially mine.

CHAPTER 14

CAITLIN

*T*he inside of Gabe's parents' house is even more stunning than the outside. There are antiques everywhere—big, heavy, wooden furniture covered in intricate carvings, statues on pedestals with names scratched into their bases that make me think they're originals, delicate lace doilies decorating claw foot couches and chairs, and so many oil paintings there's hardly a clear place on the walls.

I feel like I'm in a museum, and I'm pretty sure I would have been too afraid to sit down on any of the furniture if Gabe's mom hadn't looped her arm through mine and guided me to a blue velvet couch in the corner of the dining room, overlooking the gardens at the back of the home.

I barely have time to absorb the fact that a servant—a real servant, in a pale blue uniform dress with a white starched apron—is setting the long, mahogany table, before I am smothered by another hug from Gabe's mom and peppered with excited questions.

"So how old are you, Caitlin? Where are you going to school? What do you want to do with the rest of your life? What are your hopes and dreams," she says, pausing to dazzle me with a very white smile. "Tell me all about yourself."

"Oh…okay." I cast a frantic glance at Gabe's back as he leaves the room, wondering what I've gotten myself into. To say Gabe's mom isn't what I was anticipating is like saying a South Carolina summer is a tad warm.

Instead of the cool reserve I'd expected from an obscenely wealthy woman with a pedigree that stretches back to the Civil War, Deborah is warm, welcoming, and seems thrilled with Gabe's choice of girlfriend. She doesn't cast disparaging looks at my cheap sundress, or lift a brow at my nails that haven't seen a manicure since my sister gave me one at home for my sixteenth birthday. She doesn't wrinkle her nose when I tell her I'm working full time to take care of my younger brothers and niece, but that I'm hoping to attend college in the future. She only nods sympathetically, her dark blond bob swinging above her shoulders as her ice blue eyes— like Gabe's eyes, but without the hard edges—fill with compassion.

"That's a lot of responsibility," she says. "Especially for someone so young."

I start to shrug, but stop myself, feeling like the casual gesture would be out of place in these surroundings. "It is, but it's worth it. I want to keep my family together, and give the kids more stability than I had when I was growing up."

She sighs and her eyes begin to glisten. "Gabe is lucky to have you. I'm so glad you came into his life, Caitlin."

I swallow, not sure how to respond to her words or the emotion making her voice tremble. Gabe warned me that his mom was eager to see him settled down, but I didn't think I'd be dealing with tears of gratitude.

Mercifully, Gabe and his father enter the dining room a moment later, sparing me the stress of formulating a reply. As soon as I see the two men together, it's obvious where Gabe gets his striking good looks. He has his mother's eyes, but he has his father's chiseled cheekbones, broad shoulders, and lean, athletic build. Mr. Alexander looks pretty amazing for a guy pushing sixty—attractive, fit, with a full head of graying brown hair, and clear, intelligent, blue eyes a shade darker than his wife's and son's.

The contrast between Gabe's dad and mine is even more striking than the difference between our houses. I know Chuck is a few years younger than Mr. Alexander, but he looks a decade his senior. Chuck's body bears testimony to every bad choice he's ever made, while Mr. Alexander oozes health and wealth in a way even his wife doesn't quite manage.

Deborah's clothes are clearly expensive and her

hair intricately highlighted, but there's something fragile about her, something delicate and breakable that makes me want to punch Gabe for rolling his eyes when he sees his mother wiping tears from her cheeks.

"Mother, please," he says, a hard note in his voice. "You promised."

"I know, I know," she says, sniffing as she forces a smile. "I'm just so excited for you, honey. Caitlin is adorable. Inside and out."

"She is. She's too good for me." Gabe glances down at me with a look that banishes the urge to punch him, a look that says he means it, and that he wants more from our relationship than someone who will steal things with him.

I know it's just pretend, but the look, combined with the lingering effects of the kiss we shared in the car, make it easy to smile up at him and say, "That's ridiculous. You're exactly as good as I want you to be."

"But no better," Gabe says with a wink that makes my skin tingle, despite the fact that his parents are watching us.

I can't help it, and I can't quit replaying our kiss, over and over again. All through the introduction to his father, and the small talk the four of us exchange while we wait for the first course to be brought out, I'm thinking about Gabe's lips on my neck and the way he touched me through my dress.

Once we get to the table, things are even worse. Gabe sits next to me, close enough for him to rest his hand on my leg under the tablecloth, teasing his fingers up and down the inside of my thigh, sending agonizing currents of longing coursing through my body. I have to fight to concentrate on the dinner conversation, struggle to get my salad to my mouth without dropping lettuce on the tablecloth.

I don't know what's happening to me, only that I have never wanted anyone the way I want Gabe. I want him to touch me the way he did before, to feel his fingers sliding beneath the waistband of my panties, pushing inside where I'm already wet and aching for him. I should be ashamed of myself for wishing Gabe would finger me during a family dinner, but I'm not. The strength of my wanting leaves no room for shame, only desire and determination.

By the time dessert arrives—a chocolate mousse with fresh raspberries—my mind is made up. Screw the promise I forced from Gabe and all the reasons why it's a bad idea to get in any deeper with a boy who is a walking, talking contradiction. A boy with secrets, bad habits, a wicked way with words, and a confident touch that leaves no doubt he's *way* more experienced than I am.

I want him, and I'm going to have him.

I've spent my life putting aside my own needs and cleaning up after other people's mistakes. I want to make a mistake of my own. I know I'm playing with fire, but right now, I don't care.

Right now, I'm ready to beg to be burned.

The moment dinner is over, and Gabe and I have

wished his parents a good night and stepped outside, I reach for his hand, squeezing his fingers tight as we walk to his car.

"I don't want to go home," I say, heart racing. "I want to be alone with you."

"I've already thought of a place," he says, proving we're of like minds as he pulls me in to whisper his next words against my throat. "All I could think about the entire dinner is how much I want to taste you. I want my mouth between your legs as much as I want to keep breathing. I'm going to make you come so hard you see stars."

I shiver, despite the hot, humid night, but before I can think of what to say, Gabe opens the passenger's door and guides me inside the Beamer, his hand firm on my arm. Even that innocent touch is enough to make my pulse race faster.

Faster and faster, until I can hear my heart beating in my ears as we pull away from Darby Hill.

CHAPTER 15

CAITLIN

It is a long road that has no turning. -Irish proverb

The ride to Mr. Alexander's office seems to take forever, an eternity in which I can think of nothing but the hunger in Gabe's voice when he said he was going to make me come so hard I'd see stars.

I can't keep my eyes off where his hands grip the wheel—his big hands, with the wide palms and those elegant fingers. I bite my lip, remembering the way it felt to have those fingers moving inside me, belly fluttering as I wonder what it will feel like to have his mouth take their place.

"Are you sure you don't want me to take you home?" Gabe asks, turning left toward downtown. "I don't want to be accused of breaking my promises."

"Do you want to take me home?"

"Hell, no," he says, voice husky. "I want you to put your hand down your panties."

My breath hitches. "What?"

"I want you to touch yourself," he says, glancing my way, the heat in his eyes enough to make me feel flushed all over. "You've done that before, right?"

I swallow. "I'm twenty years old. What do you think?"

"Show me how you do it," he says, slowing the car a few miles per hour, making something inside me send up a wail of frustration, angry that he's costing us precious seconds. "Touch yourself for me, Caitlin."

My heart lurches, and my hand trembles as I reach for the hem of my dress. I'm shocked by how turned on I am, and even more shocked that I want to obey Gabe's order. That I want to lift my skirt up around my waist with one hand as I slip the other—slowly, slowly, knowing Gabe's watching out of the corner of his eye as he drives—down the front of my white satin panties.

My throat tightens and my eyes slide closed as I ease my fingers through my swollen folds, feeling the molten slickness of my own arousal, trembling as one knuckle brushes over my clit, sending a ripple of excitement sweeping through me, making my nipples tighten inside my bra. A part of me is mortified that I'm doing this in front of Gabe—especially while he's still fully dressed—but another part of me is already flying, loving the rush that sweeps through me as he curses beneath his breath. The desire in his voice makes me feel powerful, beautiful, fierce and lovely, and in touch with the most primal part of myself—like dancing, only better.

So much better.

"I can't wait to taste you," he says, his voice ragged.

My eyes squeeze more tightly closed, my breath coming faster as I dip my hand lower, dipping into the well of heat between my legs.

"Fuck it," he says. "I don't want to wait."

His fingers close around my wrist and my eyes fly open. He tugs my hand from my panties, bringing it to his mouth, slipping my index finger between his lips and suckling, moaning as his tongue sweeps up and down, licking my arousal from my skin. The firm pressure of his tongue and the light suction of his mouth send a jolt of excitement speeding through me.

I've never thought of a finger as an erogenous zone, but in Gabe's mouth, it is. It feels like every nerve-ending in my body has relocated to my finger and every one of them is celebrating being closer to Gabe's lips, his tongue, his teeth that drag lightly over my skin as he pulls one finger from his mouth only to insert the next.

He licks me clean with a thoroughness that makes it clear he loves the way I taste before threading his fingers through mine and squeezing tight.

"This is it." He swings the car into a deserted parking lot, into a space marked "Reserved for the Law Offices of Aaron Alexander."

He brakes hard; my pulse leaps in my throat.

This is it. We're here.

We slam out of the car and Gabe takes my hand, leading the way toward a white door with red trim. He punches a code into a number panel beside the door before jerking it open and half dragging me up a long, narrow flight of stairs. Our feet pound on the polished wood, mimicking the thudding of my heart against my ribs, and all of a sudden, everything feels so much more real than it did in the soft darkness of the car.

I'm really here with a boy I barely know—a boy I'm not even sure I like, at least not completely—and I'm really going to let him do things to me that I've never let anyone do. After only a few kisses and a fake date, I'm going to tear down walls I've kept firmly in place for years. It's crazy, out of character, and, if I'm not careful, I just might prove to be more like my big sister than I ever dreamed.

Anxiety dumps into my bloodstream, fear that I'm getting ready to do something I'll regret, something I will never be able to take back, no matter how much I want to, making me freeze at the top of the stairs. I'm parting my lips to tell Gabe I've changed my mind when he turns, cupping my face in his hands.

"Don't be scared," he says, as if he can read my

mind. "You can trust me." He holds my gaze as he draws me across the room. "I swear you can."

I catch glimpses of a small desk, a larger one, and some sort of sitting area in the far corner, but it's hard to focus on anything but Gabe—Gabe's lips, his breath mingling with mine, his fingertips digging lightly into my neck as we kiss.

He spins me in a half circle and the backs of my legs hit the couch, my knees almost buckling before I steady myself. "Gabe, wait I—"

"You don't have to touch me. We don't have to fuck," he says, hands sliding down to squeeze my hips through my dress. "This won't go any further than you want it to. I just want to taste you, Caitlin. I've been dreaming about it since that night in your friend's car."

Before I can tell him I've been dreaming about it too, his mouth covers mine and his tongue slips between my lips and we're kissing the way Gabe and I kiss. Like it's the last, best thing we'll ever do. Like our lives depend on getting closer, kissing deeper; like there is nothing that matters but this moment and the pleasure we can steal from it.

Pretty soon I forget my nerves, forget the reasons this is a bad idea, forget everything but the way he makes me feel shot through with lightning. I shove his suit coat off, digging my fingers into his shoulders as I lean back, pulling him down onto the couch. We fall onto the cool leather, Gabe on top, his hands smoothing up my bare legs as we continue to kiss like it's the only thing that matters.

He urges my thighs around his waist and his hard on presses between my spread legs, making me cry out because it feels so good. So good, so right, so thrilling to know I've made him this way. I've cracked his cool exterior, made him crazy with wanting me, made his breath catch, and a wild, feral sound rumble low in his throat as I lift my hips, grinding my heat against him through our clothes.

He cusses against my lips and a moment later my dress is off, and my bra, too. They are simply on my body one second and gone the next, without me remembering shifting to help Gabe dispose of them.

"You're beautiful." He sits back on his heels, eyes flicking up and down my body, a pained expression on his face. "You really are."

"You're not bad yourself," I say, reaching for his tie and working the knot free.

"No," he says, capturing my hands in his larger one. "If I take anything else off, I won't stop until it's all off. And that's not what tonight is about."

"What is tonight about?" I ask, a shockwave of desire rocketing through me at the thought of Gabe and I naked together, though I know I'm not ready, not really, no matter what the lustful voices in my head are trying to tell me.

"It's about convincing you I'm the best way to spend your summer." His palms mold to my ribs as he kisses down my neck to the hollow of my throat, soft, hot kisses that make me gasp for breath and my nipples pucker in the cool, conditioned air.

He keeps trailing kisses down the center of my

chest while his hands come to cup my breasts, holding one gently in each hand, carefully avoiding the places where I'm dying for him to kiss me, touch me. He continues to kiss me everywhere but there, his soft lips feathering back and forth across my ribs until my nipples are pulled so tight the sensation is almost painful.

Only then—when I'm squirming and moaning and there can be no doubt in his mind how much I crave his attention—does he take me in his mouth.

I cry out, driving my fingers into his hair and fisting tight, urging him closer as he licks and sucks and bites. *Bites.*

But even the biting is perfect, a flash of pain that adds to my pleasure until my breath comes fast and the world goes soft and red at the edges and there is nothing but his mouth and his tongue and the way I ache for him, burn for him, need him to spread me wide and do whatever he wants to do to me as long as he takes the ache away.

"Please, Gabe," I breathe, clawing at his shoulders. "Please."

"Please what?" he says, flicking his tongue across my nipple, making me flinch and cry out again. "You know what I like, Caitlin. You know I like you to beg for it."

"Please fuck me with your mouth," I say, the words spilling out without hesitation or anger. I'm too far gone to care what he wants me to do, so long as he gives me what I need. "Please make me come, Gabe, please. Please!"

"Lift your hips," he says, his voice tight as his fingers fist in the sides of my panties.

I obey and Gabe makes my underwear vanish and then he is between my legs, spreading my thighs with his warm hands, mumbling something I can't make out, but that sounds pained and reverent and sweet all at the same time.

As sweet as the first kiss he places to the center of me, one sweet, warm, tender kiss that threatens to unravel me completely. And then the kiss becomes a swirl of his tongue and sparks shoot from my core, sizzling across my skin, and my head feels like it's going to float right off my body and there is no more "me" to unravel, only a quivering mass of heat and need that arches closer to Gabe's mouth, shamelessly begging for what I crave.

I bite my lip and squeeze my eyes shut, not knowing what to do with all the things he's making me feel, all the sensation and emotion and the fear that I'm spiraling so far out of control I may never be the same again.

I only know that this is beautiful and wicked and perfect and I'm higher than I've ever been before. Higher than when Isaac and I sneak Irish whiskey into the midnight movie in his flask. Higher than the times I used to smoke up with Aoife, back when I was thirteen and she was seventeen and I wanted so badly to be grown up, to be old enough to start my own big adventure, the way she had started hers.

But my big adventure never came.

Instead I got big responsibility and bigger bills and the weight of an entire family on my shoulders when I was still too young to vote. Instead, I got to lock up all my longing for new things and fresh experiences and stick to choices that were safe for my family.

Now, that's all falling apart, my resolve crumbling to pieces in this man's hands. Now, there is Gabe and his kiss and his smile and the way he looks at me like I'm the most beautiful, fascinating thing he's ever seen. Gabe, who dreams about giving me pleasure, and is more than delivering on his promise to make me see stars.

By the time he cups my bottom in his hands and pulls me even closer, burying his face between my legs with a moan, I'm so close to the edge that the slight vibration is enough to send me over. I come with a ragged cry, back arching as I reach down to fist my hands in his hair, holding him close as my orgasm rips through me in long, rending waves, tightening my belly until it almost hurts, but doesn't because this is exactly what I needed.

I float back to earth so blissed out I hardly know who I am. I can't remember the last time I felt so stress free, so light and happy and flat out thrilled to be alive. And it's all because of him.

Him. Gabe, the boy who's shattered my carefully ordered world, and is cradling me amongst the wreckage.

CHAPTER 16

CAITLIN

Face the sun, but turn your back to the storm. —Irish proverb

"I want to see that smile every day." Gabe's voice penetrates the pleasure haze, making my eyes flick open.

I glance down between my thighs to see Gabe pushed up onto his elbows, watching me with an intensity that's unnerving, especially considering I'm still spread wide in front of him. I cross my arms self-consciously over my breasts and start to bring my legs together, but he stops me with two fingers on my right thigh.

"Don't," he says softly. "Not yet."

I let my thigh fall slowly back open, shocked to find a hint of desire whispering through me as I move. I wouldn't have thought it was possible to get turned on again after coming so hard my bones are still mush, but apparently…

"I want to make you come every day, at least once a day," he continues, tracing a lazy pattern on my thigh with his fingertip. "I want to give you the best summer of your life, and by the end of it, I want you to have enough money that you won't have to work when you go back to school."

"Why?" I ask, my voice deeper, huskier. "Why do you want to help me?"

"Because I like you." He meets my gaze, a vulnerable look in his eyes that makes me think he's telling the truth. "I think you're smart and kind and hardworking and the sort of person who deserves better than the hand you've been dealt." His lips lift on one side in a lopsided smile. "And you've got a delicious naughty side, and I like stealing things with you."

I take a deep breath, trying to think clearly despite the fact that I'm naked and the feel of Gabe's fingers teasing across my thigh is making me tingle all over. "What's in it for you? Aside from the fact that you get off on breaking the law?"

"I also get off on turning the tables," he says. "On lifting someone like you up, while tearing the bad guys down."

He pauses, gaze shifting back between my legs. "And I get off on you. It's killing me not to be inside you right now."

I try to bring my knees together again, but he stops me with a hand on each thigh, spreading me wider, making my breath catch.

"No," he whispers. "Stay. I like it."

"You like to torture yourself?"

"Sometimes." He sighs, a sad sound. "But next time I want more, even though I know it's a bad idea."

"It is," I agree. "For me. But I thought one night stands were your thing."

"Where did you hear that?" he asks, looking amused.

I cross my arms farther, covering more of my bare chest. "Sherry did some asking around at the club. Her friend tends bar there. He said you leave with a different girl every time you come in."

"Not since the night I left with you," he says.

My eyebrows pull together, and I do my best to ignore the way my pulse is picking up, responding to the feel of his thumbs pressing into my thighs. "So what? I'm supposed to believe you're falling for me, or something?"

"Maybe" he says in a humorless tone. "Which is stupid because I can't get involved with anyone right now. And I can't promise you more than the summer, no matter how much I might want to."

"I never asked you to promise me anything," I say, so flustered I don't know what else to say.

A part of me is glad tonight means more to him than just another one night stand—it certainly does to me. I'm not in love by any stretch, but I had fun with Gabe tonight. I enjoyed hanging out with him and could quickly become addicted to his kisses, his touch, to the way he makes me feel beautiful and special and able to relax and let go for the first time in my life. He's unpredictable, but I feel safe when he touches me.

Considering he's the most dangerous thing to enter my life since Aoife ran off, taking her drug dealer connections with her, it makes no sense, but it's true. I feel safe with Gabe, and even safer knowing all he wants is the summer. I can't very well turn into my sister or mom if Gabe's leaving at the end of August.

We can have three months, a summer to run wild and indulge all the crazy ways he makes me feel, and then Gabe will go back to school, and I'll go back to being the person I was before…except with money, and options.

The thought of being able to go to school without juggling two jobs at the same time is a heady one, but there's still one major problem—

"You said you could promise that I won't get caught," I say. "How will you manage that?"

"First of all, we'll be careful," he says, watching his finger trace swirls on my skin. "We're both smart, so that shouldn't be hard. We'll take our time and plan and practice and look at a potential job from all angles. And then, if something unexpected happens, and luck isn't on our side, I take full responsibility."

"How?" I ask. "Say you were blackmailing me or something?"

"Blackmail could work, and they'd probably let you off easy if you testified against me." He leans in pressing a kiss to my thigh that makes me shiver. "Or we act like it's a hostage situation, which would be best for you. If we can manage it."

"Either way, you're going to jail," I say, not understanding why that doesn't seem like a bigger deal to him. "I mean, not even your dad can get you out of trouble if you're caught red handed and I testify against you."

He shrugs. "Maybe, maybe not. It's a risk I'm willing to take."

"Why?" I ask again, something still not adding up. "I don't—"

"You ask too many questions." He kisses my thigh, higher this time, close enough to more intimate things that I lose my words. "We're not going to get caught. You're worrying about something that's never going to happen."

"You can't know…" My words trail away as his lips reach their destination and he kisses me again.

He kisses and licks and teases his tongue in and out of where he's already made me ache, and pretty soon I forget everything but the way he makes me feel. I forget all my questions, all my fears and worries. By the time I've left my body a second time and finally floated back down to earth, I'm too wrung out to ask questions, to do anything but lie heavily on the couch, catching my breath.

"Be right back, beautiful." Gabe brushes his knuckles tenderly across my cheek before bounding to his feet.

He covers me with a brown, fake fur throw

draped over the other end of the couch, before crossing the room and disappearing through a door on the other side of the office. I hear water running and let the sound lull me as I snuggle beneath the sinfully soft blanket. I know I should get dressed, but I'm too exhausted and satisfied to move a muscle.

Well…*mostly* satisfied.

Even after two orgasms, I'm shocked to find I still want more. I want Gabe. I want to touch him the way he's touched me. I want him naked, his stunning body bare to me, his skin hot against mine. I want to make him feel all the amazing things he made me feel. I know I'm not as experienced as he is, but I want to at least try to give him the same peace and pleasure he's given me.

When he comes back through the bathroom door a few minutes later, I sit up, holding the blanket around my breasts as I crook one finger in his direction. "Your turn."

Gabe smiles and even in the dim office light I can see that increasingly familiar spark of trouble flash in his eyes. "Not tonight. I told you, tonight is about you."

"But I feel guilty. I want to make you feel good, and, I mean, isn't it painful if a guy gets too…you know, and then doesn't…" I wave a hand vaguely in the air. "You know?"

Gabe chuckles. "I just ate your pussy for half an hour and you're embarrassed to ask if my balls are going to ache if I don't come?"

My cheeks heat as I roll my eyes. "I'm not embarrassed, I'm just…"

"Embarrassed," he finishes, amusement in his voice. "Don't be. And don't feel guilty. I took care of myself in the bathroom. Wasn't sure I'd be able to keep from taking things further if I didn't. I think I'm in love with your pussy. It's fucking beautiful and delicious. My favorite ever."

"Oh," I say, not sure how to respond. "Well… thank you."

Gabe laughs, a real, hearty laugh that echoes through the relatively small office.

"Whatever!" I reach for my bra. "I didn't know what to say. I'm not used to situations like this. I told you, I don't date."

"Good." He crosses to the larger desk a few feet from the couch and starts up the computer. "Let's keep it that way. This summer, it's you and me, no other distractions."

I narrow my eyes, watching his face in the blue light of the computer screen as I slip into my bra beneath the blanket and reach for my dress. "Does that go for you, too?"

He grins, but keeps his eyes on the screen. "Yes, Caitlin. Me, too. I want you to be my girl for the summer. Can we go steady?"

I pull my dress over my head with a laugh. "Only if you give me your class ring."

"I'll get it when I go home later tonight, and give it to you first thing tomorrow," he says, motioning me over with a hand. "Now, come look at this. I did some digging around after our last job and found this guy. I think you're going to be excited about giving him what's coming to him."

"Why's that," I ask, stepping into my panties and pulling them up before padding barefoot around the desk to stand beside Gabe.

"Read the file." He puts his arm around my waist, drawing my back to his front with an ease that feels right.

I melt into him, bringing my hand to his arm and tracing my fingers back and forth as I glance down at the screen. I've never had this kind of easy intimacy with a boy before—and Gabe is the last person I would have expected to make cuddling feel natural—but it feels right to be like this with him.

Even when I begin to read, and shock becomes rage and disgust, I don't want to pull away from Gabe. I want to get closer, to put our heads together and whisper until we've come up with a plan to make the son of bitch who's been making my brother's life a living hell for the past year pay.

"I'm in," I say, even before I've scrolled down to the second page.

"I had a feeling you would be." Gabe kisses my neck, humming happily against my skin. "I'll bring dinner to your place tomorrow night and we can talk logistics after the kids are asleep. Burgers and fries acceptable?"

"Burgers and fries will make you a hero." I turn in his arms and hook my wrists around his neck, pulling him down for a kiss.

There's no point in keeping Gabe from the kids now. They've already met my "date" and if Gabe and I are going to be spending the summer together, they might as well get used to me having a guy visiting the house. I'll just make sure everyone knows our new friend Gabe will only be around until August, and warn the kids not to get too attached.

It's not the kids you have to worry about.

I ignore the voice of doom and tilt my head, moaning as Gabe deepens our kiss. I'm not going to get attached. Gabe is fun, sexy, and a much better person than I expected him to be, but I'm not like my parents or my sister. I'm not an addict. I know when to say when. I can put the bottle down when I've had enough and not take another drink. I'll be able to do the same with Gabe come August.

But until then, I intend to have a summer to remember.

CHAPTER 17

GABE

And when Love speaks, the voice of all the gods
Makes heaven drowsy with the harmony. –Shakespeare

I'm more excited about bringing burgers over to Caitlin's house than I've been about anything in longer than I can remember.

All day Sunday—while I indulge my parents, joining them for church and lunch afterward, before spending the afternoon compiling research on the aptly named Mr. Pitt—I can't keep a smile from my face. Every once in a while I realize how ridiculous I'm being and logic does its best to drag me down into the gloom I've been inhabiting for the past few months, but the idiotic euphoria is immune to logic.

By five o'clock I'm beginning to think my mother is right: a girl is the answer to everything that ails me. Getting swept up in Caitlin won't change the facts, but if it makes me immune to the emotional side effects of my downward spiral...

Well, isn't that almost the same thing?

The Buddha said that humans are the result of all the things we've thought. The mind is everything, and what we think is what we become. If that were true in the literal sense, I'd still be back in school getting my degree, not doing my best to right a few of my father's wrongs before I break it to Mom and Dad that I won't be returning to the university. But maybe it's true in a different way. Maybe it's true in the sense that the present is all there truly is. No matter how I'm shaped by my past, or long for the future, *now* is all I have.

And right now, seeing Caitlin again is enough to keep a smile on my face.

I leave Darby Hill early, taking the time to drive through downtown to the south side of Giffney, where Morris Brothers and Sons and Daughters and Sons—one of the oldest restaurants in South Carolina, passed down through the Morris family for four generations—stands on the outskirts of the historic district. Morris Brothers has the best burgers I've ever eaten, so succulent and perfectly spiced I suspect someone in the family made a deal with the devil for the recipe.

I'm sure the kids would be fine with McDonald's, but I want to bring Caitlin the best. I want her to have the best cheeseburger while we plot our job, and I want to take her out to celebrate someplace posh as soon as we make our first deposit to her college fund. We'll hire a babysitter, eat an amazing dinner, go to a club and dance like no one is watching, and then spend the night at a hotel, fucking like no one is listening.

It sounds like a night made in heaven.

All day, I've been replaying every moment of that hour we spent on the couch. She was so beautiful—not just her lovely body, or the sexy sounds she made when I made her come—but the way she gave herself to the moment, letting go and trusting I would be there to catch her. She was every bit as wild and abandoned as I'd hoped she'd be, and she's already so deep under my skin I'd have to perform surgery to get her out.

The girl…destroys me. Just thinking about her is enough to get me hard.

By the time I get to her house with the burgers I'm pitching my fifteenth tent of the day, and am forced to sit in the car with the air conditioning blasting for several long minutes, waiting for my cock to get the message that now isn't the time.

But soon. Definitely soon.

Maybe even tonight, after the kids have gone to bed. We can make our plans, plot out our timeline, and then fuck on top of all the evidence of Mr. Pitt's crime. The crime he got away with, thanks to my father, a man who feels no moral conflict about going to church in the morning, then sitting down to strategize how to keep a guilty scumbag out of prison in the afternoon.

I'm not going to become a public defender the way I planned, or get to rub my father's nose in my contempt for the way he practices law, but I can still do something to blot the stain the Alexander family has left on this town before I leave Giffney.

And the fact that I get to do it with the beautiful girl opening her front door to wave me into the house is only going to make the summer sweeter.

"Hello, beautiful." I cross the toy-littered lawn with burgers in hand, eyes tracking up and down Caitlin's petite form as she leans against the doorframe.

In cut-off shorts, a blue-and-white-striped tank top, and bare feet, she's dressed more casually than last night, but looks even more tempting. She's sexy in a laid back way that makes me want to kiss the glistening skin at her neck, grip her ass through those faded jean shorts, and kiss each one of her moon-shaped toes where the peach polish is just starting to chip around the edges.

"No way." She stops me with a hand in the center of my chest as I lean in to kiss her. "It's too hot. I'm not getting within two feet of another person until the sun goes down."

I lift a brow. "I come bearing eight pounds of meat and five orders of curly fries and I don't even get a kiss?"

"You'll get one," she says, grinning up at me. "You'll just have to wait for it."

"I don't like to wait." I lean in again. This time she lets me get close enough to smell the soap and sweat mixing on her skin—a scent that makes my mouth water for a taste of her—before spinning away seconds before our lips touch.

"Come on," she says, laughter in her voice as she disappears into the house, clearly enjoying torturing me. "We're going to eat in the backyard. At least we'll have a breeze out there."

I follow her inside, where I'm assaulted by the smell of too many warm bodies occupying too small a space. The house didn't smell bad last night—just a little sour and damp, with overtones of garlic—but today's high was fifteen degrees warmer than yesterday's. The first summer heat wave is kicking off with highs in the low nineties and one hundred percent humidity, ensuring my family spent the day inside Darby Hill, where central air and heat were installed forty years ago.

I can't imagine anyone living through a South Carolina summer without air conditioning, but apparently Caitlin and her family intend to try.

"You do *have* air conditioning," I say, glancing around the house, looking for a thermostat. "This house isn't that old."

"We have it, we just can't afford to turn it on," she says, kicking toys out of her path as she makes her way through the living room and into the kitchen. She snags a pitcher of tea from the fridge and sets it on the counter before beginning to fill a blue plastic tray with glasses. "Sorry for the mess. I've been working with Ray on a project for school and Sean and Emmie didn't clean up the toys like I asked."

"I couldn't care less about the mess," I say. "But it's fucking miserable in here."

She turns back to me with a falsely sympathetic look. "Oh, poor baby. Don't worry; you won't melt. You're not that sweet."

"But you are." I grin as I reach out, snagging her ponytail and giving it a tug as I push her against the refrigerator, dropping my lips to the sweat-slick skin of her throat. "In fact, I think you're already melting." I kiss up her neck toward her ear, growling when she pushes me away.

"I'm serious, psycho," she says with a laugh. "No body heat in my vicinity until it's dark, and at least ten degrees cooler."

"Turn on the air conditioning," I say, hungry for another taste of her. "I'll pay for it."

She wags her finger back and forth with a smile. "None of that. I don't want you paying for things. I want to be an empowered lady thief."

"You're in a good mood," I say, loving how much more relaxed she seems today. "Impending crime agrees with you."

"Revenge agrees with me." She casts a glance down the hall leading toward the back of the house before turning back to me. "You won't believe all the things I found out about Mr. Pitt today. I called my friend Jenny who works part time in the office at the junior high. At first she didn't have much to say, but then I told her how many times I've been called in for meetings since Danny's been in Pitt's class and she starting spilling her guts. Everyone hates this guy. *Everyone*. I can't believe he still has a job."

I frown. "You shouldn't have talked to anyone. We don't want this woman remembering you asked questions about Pitt. Once the police start investigating, it could lead them your way."

Caitlin shakes her head as she fetches ice from the freezer and plunks it into the glasses. "No seriously, *everyone* hates him, Gabe. There will be dozens of suspects, and I was careful. I never asked Jenny any direct questions, just led her around to talking about what I wanted to talk about."

She finishes with the ice and starts grabbing silverware from a drawer overflowing with no less than a hundred mismatched utensils, a chaotic collection that would give my mother nightmares.

"Besides," she continues, "Jenny's a friend. She wouldn't rat me out, even if she thought I had something to do with the robbery. Which she wouldn't, because she knows I won't even sneak into a movie without paying."

I swipe sweat from my forehead, wishing I'd known I was going to be eating dinner in the seventh level of hell before I decided to wear jeans. "All right, but next time, no talking to friends, or anyone else. We keep this between you and me. If we don't talk to anyone but each other, then we know no one will talk to the police."

"All right. Makes sense." She shoves a roll of

napkins my way before scooping up the tray. "Speaking of you and me, the kids are pretty keyed up about me having a boyfriend. It's crazy. I didn't expect it to be that big of a deal, but I guess our lives are just *that* boring."

"You told them I was your boyfriend?" I ask, stupidly pleased.

"Just for the summer," she says, leading the way down the hall and through what looks like a combination play room/mud room, where trunks full of blocks and stuffed animals war for space with an overflowing coat rack next to a mountain of muddy shoes. "I told them you're going back to college, so it's not serious."

"Who said I was going back to college?"

She pauses, glancing back at me. "Aren't you?"

"Doubtful," I say. "But I do have other unbreakable plans."

She nods, a shadow crossing her face for a moment before she smiles even more brightly than before. "Right, so I told them it was only for the summer, but Sean and Ray are already talking about where you're going to drive them in your fancy car, and Danny has decided you're the Anti-Christ."

I move ahead of her, holding the back door open. "And why's that?"

"He says you make eye contact like a psychopath," she says, with a shrug as she ducks under my arm. "I told him that's the kind of eye contact I like, and to shut up and be nice, but I'm not sure he's going to be civil. Just so you're warned."

I nod, glancing up to find Danny already glaring at me from the far side of the lawn, where the three Cooney boys are kicking a soccer ball while Emmie scoots through the middle of their game on a plastic train.

"Well, maybe Morris Brothers burgers will change his mind."

"You're kidding." Caitlin turns to me with wide eyes, glancing from me to the bag, smile spreading as she backs across the lawn. "I thought I smelled something more delicious than Dave's Drive In. You went for the good stuff!"

"For you? Always," I say, enjoying the way she looks both pleased and flustered by the compliment before she turns to shout—

"Food's here! Rinse your hands in the hose if they're muddy and come and get it!"

Moments later, I'm surrounded by hot, grass-and-sweat scented bodies pressing in close as I set the bag of food down on the picnic table and begin divvying up the goods. Ray slips onto the seat beside me on one side, Sean on the other, while Caitlin gets Emmie settled and starts handing out cups and pouring sweet tea. Danny is the last to join the group—settling onto the edge of the opposite seat, as far from me as he can get—but his glare fades as soon as he gets a cheeseburger in his mouth. He doesn't join the conversation or ask to come along for the ride I promise to give Sean and Ray after dinner, but he's civil, and even laughs when Caitlin teases him about having a tape worm, saying it's the only explanation for how he can eat three times as much as anyone else in the family and stay so skinny.

The meal takes approximately fifteen minutes—about five times faster than any meal ever eaten in the Alexander home—and then the kids are up playing again and Caitlin and I are alone at the table, surrounded by ketchup-streaked burger wrappers and a few lone fries that escaped being devoured whole.

"Thanks for bringing dinner," she says, resting her sweating glass of sweet tea against her cheek for a moment before taking a sip.

"You're welcome." I watch her throat work as she drinks, wondering how she can make even sipping tea look sexy. "It was fun."

"It was." She grins. "You're good with the kids."

"You sound surprised."

"I am, a little." She lifts one bare, lightly freckled shoulder. "You don't have any brothers or sisters. It's not like you've had a lot of practice dealing with small people."

"Small people are just people," I say. "But smaller. With less bullshit to cut through to find out what they're really about."

"True," she says, casting a glance in the kids' direction before adding in a softer voice, "Speaking of bullshit, I'm supposed to have a conference with Pitt tomorrow. I don't know how I'm going to keep from slapping him."

"What's the conference for?"

"Same thing they've been about all year—Danny's lack of respect for his elders." She rolls her eyes. "I mean, it's no wonder. My mom and dad didn't exactly instill a lot of confidence in the older generation. Danny's other teachers have always understood that, and taken the time to work with Danny, earn his trust." She shakes her head. "But I swear Mr. Pitt *deliberately* pushes Danny's buttons. It's like he wants to see him fail."

"Maybe he does," I say. "Seems like he enjoys tormenting the people he has under his thumb."

Caitlin leans closer. "I was thinking about that today, that Pitt must have enjoyed what he did to his mother. Otherwise, why keep her alive for so many years? Why not 'accidentally' give her the wrong amount of medication right away?"

"I agree. If he was after the house and the inheritance, there was no reason to spend nearly a decade sliding meals through a slot in the door and emptying the pot he gave her to piss in."

"What a fucking monster." Caitlin's eyes darken, and rage hardens her features, giving her beauty a cold edge that makes me want to kiss her even more. "I can't believe he didn't go to jail. Even if the jury was convinced the overdose was an accident, how did they excuse keeping an elderly woman with diabetes and mental problems locked in an attic for *eight years* just because Pitt didn't want to pay for the kind of care she needed?"

I shrug. "Elder abuse is notoriously hard to prove. Almost no one gets convicted, which is why my father took the case in the first place. Even though he knew Pitt was a murderer."

Caitlin shakes her head. "How does your dad sleep at night?"

"Very well," I say, with a smile. "It's my mother who's addicted to sleeping pills."

"No, seriously, Gabe," she says. "Your dad seemed nice yesterday. Meeting him, you'd never think he was the kind of person who would defend all these horrible people."

"I don't know." I grab Ray and Sean's discarded burger wrappers and wad them into a ball before throwing them back into the bag. "I guess he's done the mental gymnastics to make it acceptable."

"That sounds familiar." Caitlin sighs, eyes dropping to the graying wood of the picnic table. "I've been doing some mental gymnastics the past few days…"

I cover her hand with mine. "But our gymnastics are the right gymnastics."

"Are they?" She threads her fingers through mine. "I mean, does robbing Mr. Pitt make anything better? It won't undo what happened to his mom, or keep him from bullying his students, or send him to prison where he belongs."

"You're saying the punishment doesn't fit the crime." I nod, considering her point. "So you think we should revise our plan? Arrange to have Pitt trapped in a blazing hot room with only one tiny window to look out at the world for a month or two, give him a taste of his own medicine?"

Caitlin's eyes flick sharply back to mine. "You're not serious."

"I could be," I say. "I like the idea of hitting the guy where it hurts."

She shakes her head as she detangles our fingers. "No, Gabe, I'm not—"

"Katydid, there you are!" a masculine voice booms from behind us, cutting Caitlin short.

As the color drains from her face, I turn to see an older man with salt and pepper hair, a nose with the same ski-slope shape as Caitlin's—though larger, and redder—and bloodshot eyes stumbling down the back steps. His ample stomach bounces as he misjudges the distance between the final step and the ground and he staggers sharply to the left before regaining his balance. He's wearing a stained blue tee shirt and khaki pants, paired with battered black dress shoes, and is about three spaghetti stains short of resembling the bums who gather outside my parents' church on Wednesday mornings for free breakfast.

And I suspect he is Caitlin's dad, a suspicion he confirms when he says in a slurred voice—

"Sweetheart, I have a problem. I need some help from my best girl."

I dislike him immediately, even before I turn back to see the confident, laid back Caitlin who met me at the door tonight replaced by a pale, vulnerable-looking girl with panic written clearly on her features.

CHAPTER 18

CAITLIN

A man takes a drink; the drink takes a drink;
the drink takes the man. –Irish proverb

I jump to my feet, making it around the picnic table and intercepting Dad before he gets close enough to realize there's a stranger at the table. Chuck lost his last pair of glasses months ago and can't see for shit at a distance. If I can keep him away from the table, give him whatever he wants, and send him on his way, this shouldn't have to turn ugly in front of Gabe.

As long as Chuck's not asking for money you don't have...

"Please don't be asking for money," I mutter as I cross the yard.

"There you are." Chuck grins down at me as I

hook my arm through his and turn him toward the house. "There's my best girl."

"What's up, Dad?" I lead him back across the grass, nose wrinkling at the sour, alcohol-and-garlic-infused smell rising from his clothes.

"Veronica kicked me out," he says. "She says I can't come back until I start paying room and board. I think she's serious this time. She had that look in her eye."

I sigh. It's about money. Of course it is.

What else does Chuck ever need from his "best girl?"

"Dad, I don't have anything to loan you right now," I say, though we both know this would be a *gift*, not a loan. For the past year, money has only flowed one way between Chuck and me—*from* me, *to* him. "After paying the taxes on the house, I'm strapped. And the kids are going to be out of school soon, and I'll be paying for daycare… You know that's crazy expensive."

"Aw, come on, Kit Cat, you always have a little something stashed away," Dad says, using one of his many pet names for me, the ones I used to love when I was little and thought that someone calling you a sweet name meant they loved you.

Now, I know better. Words from my dad mean less than nothing. Words are weapons Chuck uses to manipulate the people unlucky enough to be related to him.

"I really don't this time, Dad," I say, determined to stand firm. "I'm sorry."

Gabe and I haven't hit Mr. Pitt's house yet, and we may still end up calling off the job. Robbery, I can stomach, but anything else is out of the question. I didn't like the look in Gabe's eye when he talked about the punishment fitting the crime.

I liked the fact that something deep inside of me agreed with him even less. I have no intention of becoming one of the monsters in Gabe's dad's files, but Gabe and I are standing on a slippery slope, and I have a feeling it would be easier than I can imagine to slide down into the muck.

"I can't go back to sleeping on the damned couch," Chuck says, anger creeping into his tone. He wrenches his arm from mine, refusing to let me lead him the rest of the way into the house. "I've got a plate in my shoulder and a bad back. I need a bed, Kitty Cat."

I run a clawed hand through my hair, sneaking a glance back at the picnic table, grateful to see Gabe still sitting where I left him, though he's watching my exchange with Chuck like a predator debating whether or not to pounce.

I need to get this handled. ASAP.

"Okay, Dad, fine." I hate what I'm about to do, but I've got no other choice. The kids are already sharing rooms and I don't want Chuck waking them up in the middle of the night when he comes stumbling home drunk.

"You can have your old room back," I say, the words stinging on the way out. "I'll set the bunk bed back up in Danny's room, and Emmie and I can share. She's old enough to sleep in a big bed, and…I don't know, maybe I can sell the toddler bed for a few bucks."

Chuck shakes his head so hard he stumbles before regaining his balance. "I can't sleep here, Caitlin. It's too damned hot."

I open my mouth to tell him that I can turn on the air conditioning if he's willing to hand over his VA check at the beginning of the month—that check would cover air conditioning *and* an entire month of daycare, and I wouldn't mind getting my hands on it before Chuck can drink it away—but he rolls on before I can get a word in.

"I need my own space," he says, folding his arms over his belly, which has gotten even rounder since he moved in with Veronica, and started eating her Italian home cooking. "I *deserve* my own space after raising kids for twenty-four damned years."

I bite my lip, refusing to call him on his bullshit. Deep down, I think he knows that I've been doing the kid-raising around here for a long time, and Aoife was doing the heavy lifting before I was old enough, but he'd never admit it out loud. Gabe's dad has his mental gymnastics, and my father has his. Chuck's involve casting himself as the long-suffering, hard-working father, whose failures lie at the feet of the wife who left him, the children who never appreciated him, and the government who let him down.

His self-image relies on ignoring that by the time Ray and Sean were born, he was at the bar almost every night, and that for the past few years he's only seen the kids when he was drunk off his ass.

"Well, I'm sorry, Dad," I say in my Chuck voice, that calm, lulling tone good for talking down drunks and Gretchen, when she gets her apron in a twist at work. "I can offer you a bed here, but I don't have any money to spare."

He scowls, his thick brows shadowing his eyes, transforming his cheery elf face into something uglier, into that sneering mask I remember from watching my parents fight when I was little.

"You're a liar," he spits. "Just like your mother."

"I'm nothing like Mom," I say, though I know arguing with him is pointless. "I've helped you out every time I could afford to, and even sometimes when I couldn't. The last time I bailed you out with Hal it almost cost me the house."

"Cost *me* the house. It's *my* house, little girl," Chuck says, jabbing a finger in my face. "Don't forget where your bread's buttered."

I laugh, a mean laugh I can't seem to hold in. "Give me a break, Dad. I keep *your* bread buttered, not the other way around, and you know it."

"Watch your mouth." His blue eyes narrow. "I'm good to you, Caity May. Most fathers wouldn't let a full-grown girl keep hanging around, sleeping under their roof. Most fathers would tell you to get off your ass, and get your own place."

"Are you kidding me?" I sputter, fighting to keep my temper in check and losing. "You are so full of shit. You would have lost the house *and* the kids if it weren't for me."

Chuck shrugs, his mouth pulling down hard on the sides. "Well…maybe they'd be better off with the state. Maybe I should put in a call."

I see stars—white hot stars bursting at the edges of my vision—and the next thing I know I'm lunging at Chuck. I'm half my father's size, but I'm also less than half his age, stone cold sober, and angry. So fucking angry it feels like my chest is going to explode.

How *dare* he? How *dare* he threaten this family after all I've done to hold us together? It makes my bones vibrate with rage as I slam my palms into his barrel chest and shove.

I push him as hard as I can, but still, I don't expect him to go reeling backward, tripping hard over the toy truck Sean left out in the grass, and landing flat on his back. Chuck's cry of pain as he hits the ground makes me flinch and the wave of anger ebb a bit, but I'm still livid, so mad my voice shakes when I speak.

"Get out." I point a finger around the side of the house. "Get off this property, don't come back until you're sober, and don't you dare threaten this family again."

"Bitch," Chuck groans as he rolls onto his side, wincing as he moves.

"And I want the money you owe me for bailing you out with Hal," I say, refusing to let Chuck's name-calling hurt. He's called me a bitch before, and he's always sorry for it when he sobers up. He'll probably be back here tomorrow begging forgiveness for the scene he's causing today, but right now I don't care. I just want him gone.

"Selfish little bitch," he says, struggling to his feet. "You don't care about those kids. You only care about yourself!"

"That may be one of the most ludicrous things I've ever heard." Gabe sounds amused, and when he appears at my side, he looks as cool and collected as always, but I can see the tension simmering in his muscles as he steps in front of me, placing himself between me and Chuck.

I take his elbow and try to pull him back—getting in the middle of things will only make this worse—but it's too late, Chuck has already smelled blood in the water.

"And who the holy fuck is this?" he asks, eyes widening as he looks from me to Gabe and back again. "You moved your boyfriend into my house? Is that why there's suddenly no room for your own damned father?"

"She offered you a room," Gabe says. "You turned it down."

"Shut up, pretty boy," Chuck says. "You may be fucking my daughter, but that doesn't give you the right to—"

Chuck's words end in a gurgle as Gabe grabs fistfuls of Dad's spaghetti-sauce-speckled shirt, lifting my father off the ground as he spins and slams Chuck's back against the house. I gasp, hand flying to cover my mouth as I stumble a few steps away, not knowing what's more surprising—that Gabe is even stronger than he looks, or that, for the first time in my life, I can see fear on Chuck's face.

Even when Hal was threatening to beat my father's bar tab out of him if Chuck didn't pay up, the fear in Chuck's voice as he begged me to bail him out never reached his eyes. No matter how much shit he brings upon himself, my dad is the kind of person who always believes he'll be able to slither out of trouble in the end.

And why shouldn't he believe it? For fifty-three years, that's always been the case.

The fact that Gabe is the first person I've ever seen frighten my dad makes the hair on my arms stand on end, even before Gabe says in a low, menacing voice—

"You don't talk about Caitlin that way. You don't comment on our relationship, you don't critique her choices, and you don't come back here unless you've got money in your hands and an apology on your lips. Do you understand?"

Dad pulls in a breath, wincing as he exhales. "Put me down."

"Do you understand?" Gabe repeats, the muscles in his arms bunching tighter as he lifts my father higher up the side of the house.

"I've got a bad back!" Dad cries out, voice pinched.

"Do you—"

"Fuck you!" Chuck shouts, his words transforming into a howl of pain as Gabe pulls him away from the wall and slams him back into the paneling.

"Gabe stop, the kids," I say, turning to check on my brothers and Emmie.

"Don't stop because of us," Danny says in a shaky voice. He stands not far behind me, hands balled into fists at his sides. His cheeks are pale, but his eyes glitter with a cruel satisfaction I don't like seeing on his face. Not even a little bit.

"Get out of here, Danny," I say, flinching as my dad's back hits the wall a third time and his groan becomes a high-pitched yelp. "You don't need to see this. Go check on the others."

"The others are fine," Danny says, eyes glued to Gabe's back. "I'm staying."

I glance toward the rear of the yard to see that Ray has corralled Sean and Emmie into the far corner, near the hole in the fence, and is doing his best to shield them from the scene near the house. But I spot Sean's wide, frightened eyes peeking around Ray's arm and I can hear Emmie crying.

It's the sound of her tears that makes me turn and grab Gabe's arm, digging my fingers into the tightly knotted muscle. "Enough, Gabe. Put him down!"

Gabe hesitates, holding my dad's gaze for a long beat.

"The baby's crying," I say in a softer voice. "Please, just...let it go. He's not worth it."

Gabe's jaw clenches and for a second I don't think he's going to listen to me, but finally his muscles shift beneath my hand and he loosens his grip, letting Chuck slide down the wall. Dad lands in a heap, breath rushing out in a groan as his palms reach back to brace himself against the concrete foundation.

"Get out," Gabe whispers, nudging my father toward the side of the house with his shoe.

Chuck staggers to his feet, swallowing hard as he backs away. He keeps his eyes glued to Gabe, watching him like he's a bomb about to go off. Chuck doesn't glance my way until he's about to turn the corner, and then only for a moment before he stumbles away, but a moment is enough to see the hurt and shock in his eyes. Hurt and shock, with a kernel of fury at the center.

If I know my dad, it won't take long for that kernel to sizzle and pop, and for Chuck to start working out a way to make me pay for humiliating him.

"Shit." I drop my face into my hands, drawing in a deep breath that does nothing to calm the fear rising inside me.

"I'll make sure he's gone," Gabe says from beside me.

"Don't bother." I lift my face from my hands, shoving the hair from my face. "He'll leave, but he'll be back in a day or two, and everything will be worse than it was before. So…thanks a lot."

Gabe turns back, a guarded expression on his face. "You sound angry."

"I *am* angry," I say. "You should have stayed out of it. I know how to handle my father."

"I think Gabe was awesome," Danny says, excitement in his tone. "I loved that shit. I've been dying to see Chuck pinned to a fucking wall."

"Language!" I shout over my shoulder at my brother, breath huffing out as I try to regain control. "Just…go check on Emmie, okay?"

"But I—"

"Go check on Emmie." I point a finger toward the rear of the yard. "Now!"

Danny scowls and curses beneath his breath, but he turns and starts toward the corner of the fence. I shift my attention back to Gabe, forcing myself to lower my voice. "I get that you were trying to help, but my dad doesn't respond well to threats. He's going to get over being scared, and decide to get even."

Gabe takes a step closer. "How will he get even?" he asks in a mild voice that makes it difficult to believe I watched him lose it in a major way a minute ago. "Will he make you work two jobs to take care of his kids, while refusing to pay a dime to help? Come begging for money and verbally abuse you when he doesn't get what he wants?"

"Yeah, that's funny," I say in a tone I hope makes it clear I don't find it funny at all. "But you don't understand. Things can always get worse."

"In this situation, I fail to see how."

"All kinds of ways," I say. "Once, back when my

sister was in charge and she kicked Chuck out of the house for the first time, he hired a crew of guys to come rip up the front porch and leave the pieces in the yard. And then, when the men he'd hired found out Chuck couldn't pay them, they threw a rock through the living room window. We spent Christmas Day freezing to death and had to pawn Mom's last piece of good jewelry to pay for a new window."

Gabe sighs, bringing a hand to press at his temple as if this conversation is giving him a headache. But Gabe doesn't know what a headache is yet, not until he's been on the receiving end of Chuck Cooney's vengeful side.

"Another time," I continue, "right after I told him I was moving into his and Mom's old room, since he hardly ever slept here anymore, Chuck showed up at the school and told the office not to release Danny into my care. He told them he was the one with custody, and he'd be picking his son up from now on.

"He picked Danny up for exactly *two* days before he disappeared and I had to have a meeting with the principal and beg Chuck to sign a bunch of paperwork to get approved to pick my brother up again. That cost me two hundred dollars, by the way, because Chuck doesn't sign anything he isn't getting paid to sign."

"You shouldn't have paid him a dime," Gabe says.

"I didn't have a choice, don't you get that?" I ask, exasperated. "Chuck has custody of the kids. I'm not even a legal caregiver. He knows I don't have a leg to stand on if he calls the Department of Human Services like he threatened."

"But why would the state take the kids away from you? Custody or no custody?" Gabe asks. "It should be clear to anyone who takes a second to look that you're devoted to them, and they're being well-cared for."

I cross my arms, shaking my head. "When it comes to the Cooneys, DHS takes kids into custody first, and asks questions later. One time, I ended up in foster care because my mom was taking a *nap* when the DHS worker showed up. She wasn't even passed out that time, just sleeping, but the case-worker didn't care. He took me and my sister, and Danny, who was just a baby, and we all ended up in separate homes."

"I'm sorry that happened to you," Gabe says.

"I don't need you to be sorry," I say. "I need you to understand that if the state takes the kids, I won't be able to get them back without Chuck. He'll have to sign the paperwork, because he's the one with legal custody."

Gabe stares at me for a long moment, his blue eyes cool and unreadable, making me wonder if he's heard a word I've said, before he nods. "Okay, then you'll sue him for custody. My father can start the paperwork. I'll speak with him about representing you tonight."

I fight the urge to roll my eyes. "Gabe, I can't sue. I don't have that kind of money, especially not to hire your dad."

"He'll do the case pro bono," Gabe says. "He does a few of those every year, and he likes you, I can tell. He'll be glad to help."

My mouth opens and closes with no words coming out, not sure how I feel about what Gabe's suggesting. On the one hand, it feels like charity, and I don't want that from Gabe. But the thought of having the legal right to tell Chuck to stay out of our lives if he won't behave is insanely tempting. How much easier would life be if I didn't have to worry about Chuck screwing things up every time he doesn't get his way?

"She wants you." Danny appears at my side, a sniffling Emmie in his arms.

The moment I see her splotchy red face and eyelashes matted with tears, I know what I have to do. I can't let her grow up under Dad's reign of terror. He's only getting worse. The sweet Dad who used to play the fiddle for us at night, and sneak a few bucks of candy money into your pocket when you least expected it, hasn't been around in a long time. It makes me sad to know Emmie will never know that side of Chuck, but I can't keep sticking my head in the sand, and pretending things are going to be okay.

Things are only going to be okay if I make them okay and that means making sure Chuck doesn't have the power to swing a wrecking ball through this family.

"Okay." I turn back to Gabe as I stroke Emmie's back. "If your dad's okay with taking the case pro bono, I can meet with him one morning this week. Wednesday or Thursday would be best. I don't have to clock in at the diner until nine forty-five on those days."

Gabe smiles, that devilish smile that makes him even more handsome. "Unless you decide to quit."

"I can't quit."

"Can't quit *yet*," Gabe corrects with a wink before turning to the boys. "Who wants to go for a ride? I've got room for three."

"I'll come," Danny says, clearly having experienced a change of heart where Gabe is concerned. I'm not thrilled that the change was inspired by violence, but...I guess beggars can't be choosers.

"I'll go." Ray steps up beside Danny, hanging close to his big brother, the way he always does in the aftermath of a Chuck-splosion.

"Me too! Me too!" Sean's arm shoots up as he bounces on his toes, the smile on his face proving he's put the dark part of the evening behind him. But Sean is usually the swiftest to recover, and it's not like we haven't been through this with Chuck before.

The kids aren't used to seeing Dad pounded by my boyfriend, but they *are* used to seeing Dad wasted and causing trouble, doling out cuffs to the head when Danny talks back, or Ray spends too much time in the bathroom. It's the worst kind of routine, but one I haven't known how to break free of. There was never enough money or time or support for me to dream that I'd have a chance at getting custody, there was never…Gabe.

"See you soon," he says, as the boys race each other around the house to the Beamer. "I'll take them for a ride down to the old mill, and get ice cream before we head back."

"They'll drip in your car," I warn.

"It's just a car." Gabe leans down to kiss my forehead, making my chest tight, a condition that only gets worse when Emmie laughs and pats his cheek.

"She likes you."

"I like her," Gabe says, smiling at Emmie before his gaze shifts back to me and the smile becomes something more intense. "And I like you. I'll fix anything I messed up tonight, we'll finish what we started with Pitt, and everything will be fine. I promise."

"I believe you," I say, meaning it.

It scares me, but I do. I believe in Gabe, and maybe, even more dangerously, I'm starting to believe in this dreamy future he's spinning, daring to imagine what it might be like to not only survive, but to break free, and take the people I love with me.

CHAPTER 19

CAITLIN

You'll never plough a field by turning it over in your mind. –Irish proverb

I ignore the way my skin has already begun to sweat in the unrelenting heat of the June night, tug my long-sleeved black shirt down to my wrists, and pull on my gloves. The gloves are black leather, softer and suppler than anything I've ever owned.

They arrived in the mailbox yesterday, unwrapped, without a note saying who they were from, but I knew. Just like I know that Gabe will be here in exactly two minutes. He's always on time.

I have two minutes to decide this is insane, turn around, and run back to the van as fast as my legs can carry me. I know I should. But instead, I tug the back of my black sock cap lower on my neck, making sure every strand of blond hair is tucked safely beneath, before sliding the mask over my face.

As soon as the soft knit smoothes over my skin —concealing everything but my eyes and mouth—I feel something shift inside of me. The black uniform helps silence the voices warring in my head, reducing me to the simplest version of myself, the one who wants to survive and won't let anyone stand in my way. The anxiety that has followed me since I crept out of the house fifteen minutes ago vanishes, leaving cold, steady certainty in its place.

Pitt deserves this; he deserves this and more. The man tortured and abused his mother for eight years before administering a lethal overdose, all while filming the misery he was inflicting so he could relive the nightmare over and over. Now, he lives to torment the kids he's supposed to be helping, staying on as a teacher for the joy of making preteens suffer, when his inheritance was more than enough to set him up for life.

At our conference after school yesterday, Pitt threatened to fail Danny, even though his grades are all B's and C's. After spending the entire year riding Danny's ass, I would have assumed Pitt would be glad to see my brother go, but the bastard wants to keep his favorite punching bag around for another year. He said he was recommending Danny be held back to give him another year to "mature."

The only thing another year with Mr. Pitt would mature in Danny is his determination to give authority the middle finger. He wouldn't make it. He'd end up getting transferred to the alternative school, where, at thirteen, he'd be one of the youngest kids on campus. He'd either be eaten alive, or drawn into a group of kids way more dangerous and destructive than the Baker boys down the street. Either one is intolerable. I won't see Danny's life ruined because one nasty man singled him out as his latest victim.

I have a meeting with Principal Tharp to discuss whether or not Danny should be held back on Thursday. I'm hoping Pitt will have tendered his resignation by then. Without Pitt applying pressure, I know Tharp can be persuaded that holding Danny back isn't in anyone's best interests. After all, passing him means she only has to deal with his crap for one more year before he's promoted to high school, instead of two.

"Hey there." Gabe's whisper comes from the shadowed woods behind me, but it doesn't startle me.

I've been waiting to hear his voice again since we parted ways outside my house late last night, after a good night kiss that scrambled my thoughts even more than the hour spent plotting how to get in and out of Pitt's house within Gabe's ten minute time limit. I'm not sure the tapes Gabe's father's file mentioned still exist—if I were Pitt, I would have destroyed that evidence long before I went to trial—but Gabe thinks they do, and that I'll find them in the attic. He scouted the house yesterday while Pitt was at work, and says the ground floor is very sparsely furnished. There aren't many places to store a box of old, VHS surveillance tapes, and Gabe's betting Pitt is keeping the videos of his mother's suffering in the same place he kept his mother.

"Nice mask," Gabe whispers, as I turn to face the silhouette emerging from the shadows across the street from the elegant, old farmhouse where Mr. Pitt's mother was born and died. "And stunning gloves."

"Thanks, they were a gift from this boy I like." I move into his arms, blood singing as his Gabe smell fills my head and my breasts flatten against his chest. I can't make out his expression in the darkness, but I can feel how much I affect him in the way his fingers curl into my hips, pulling me closer.

"Glad they reached you safely," he says. "Any trouble on the way?"

"Nope, the kids are all asleep, and I left a note saying I was running to the Laundromat to pick up a load I forgot this afternoon in case anyone wakes up. I parked the van under the railroad trestle down the road. Only took me two minutes to get here."

"Should take less on the way back," Gabe says, a smile in his voice. "Post job adrenaline is pretty intense. You ready to go?"

"I think so." I take a breath and let it out slowly, shocked to find my heartbeat speeding only a little. Gabe and I went over the plan so many times it feels like we've already pulled this off. Now, it's just a matter of going through the motions.

"Remember, the ten minutes start as soon as you're in," Gabe whispers. "Find the tapes first, then poke around for anything valuable. I'm pretty sure the jewelry is on the ground floor in the mother's old room. It doesn't look like it's been touched since before Pitt decided to start keeping her in the attic. So I'll take care of that, but it wouldn't hurt for you to hunt for other goodies if you have time."

I nod. "And if I don't find the tapes?"

"We'll revisit the plan when we get back to your place, do some more digging, and find another way to blackmail him. But I'm betting you'll find them."

"How much are you betting?" I ask in a lilting tone, shocked that I'm flirting at a time like this.

"I'm betting dinner, dancing, and a swanky hotel room Friday night. All on me," Gabe says, giving my hips another squeeze before adding in a smoky voice, "And I promise to make you come at least three times before I let you sleep."

I press closer, the feel of him getting hard against my stomach making me ache. "And if *I* win, I'll let you teach me how to give a blow job."

Gabe's fingers dig into the curve of my bottom. "I doubt you'll need teaching."

"I might," I say, pressing up on tiptoes to press a kiss to the cleft of his chin. "I've never given one before."

His breath rushes out. "Never?"

"Never," I confirm, kissing his cheek before

moving my lips within a breath of his, hovering just out of reach as I speak. "But I want you to be my first. I've been imagining what you'll taste like since that night at your dad's office."

He groans softly, trapping my sock-cap-covered head between his hands. "Stop it. Or I'm going to take you to the van and get you naked in the back, and we're not going to leave here with any of the things we came for."

"All right." I rock back off my tiptoes and take a reluctant step away, putting distance between us. "But promise to meet me at the house later. I'll leave my window open. You can climb the tree outside, sneak in, and…stay the night if you want."

"Sounds perfect," he says, sending a sizzle of anxiety-laced-anticipation racing across my skin.

I know I should be more nervous about breaking into Pitt's place than potentially having sex with Gabe for the first time, but the events of this evening are already all mixed up together in my head. I feel like I did that night at the pawnshop, fear and attraction fusing to create a heightened state that makes me feel more awake, more alive than I've ever felt before. I can't wait to visit unto Pitt some much deserved karmic retribution, and I can't wait to feel Gabe's skin against mine, the two are tangled together and I don't care to untangle them, not when the combined stakes make the thrill that much more intense.

"I'll be back outside in ten minutes," Gabe says, squeezing my hand as we step to the edge of the shadows. "If I'm caught, I'll make enough noise for you to hear me in the attic. You'll have time to get out and make a run for it before the police arrive. It's only a thirteen-foot drop from the window. You'll be fine as long as you land with bent knees."

I nod, and impulsively lean in, giving him one last kiss on the cheek. "For luck."

"I've already used up all my luck," he says, giving my hand a gentle squeeze. "You keep it."

Before I can respond, he starts across the road. I follow, boots crunching lightly in the gravel before we hit the lawn and our footfalls go silent. I tail Gabe through the blue moonlight around to the side of the darkened house, amazed that the night is so quiet.

In my neighborhood, it's never this quiet, not even at two in the morning. There are too many people with babies, couples who brawl in the middle of the night, and people working double shifts and graveyard shifts, whatever hours they have to work to get by. There is always someone coming or going, someone shouting or laughing or crying or calling a dog or shooting a rifle into the air to scare the starlings away in the fall.

Here, at the edge of town, on a narrow dirt road where the gentlemen farmers of another age built their sprawling farmhouses, the world is silent. There is no wind tonight, no rustle of trees, not a sound except for the occasional chirp of an insect the heat hasn't lulled into a coma. The quiet is smothering, and by the time we reach the yard beneath the attic window and I crawl onto Gabe's shoulders, I'm finding it hard to breathe.

Or maybe you're just scared out of your damned mind.

My hands shake as I ease the windowpane open and pull myself up to the sill, but I'm not sure it's fear making them tremble. I'm excited too, so ready for this that I can already taste how good it's going to feel to hear Mr. Pitt won't be returning to teach seventh grade in the fall.

My biceps flex and I hook my leg over the edge of the window, hauling myself silently inside, grateful for all those heavy trays I carry at Harry's. I don't have any trouble lifting my own weight. I feel strong, confident, every cell vibrating with determination as I step down onto the dusty boards, giving my eyes a moment to adjust to the dim light.

The moment they do, my stomach clenches and the worst wave of acid I've experienced in days surges up my throat. My sour stomach has been behaving itself lately—having Gabe around seems to agree with it—but now Gabe is gone, off breaking into the ground floor.

He might as well be a hundred miles away. A million.

I suddenly feel terrifyingly alone and trapped, though I know Gabe's right and, unlike the woman held captive here before me, I'm young and fit enough to jump to freedom if Gabe doesn't come back to catch me.

But as I stare at the stained mattress lying on the

floor to the far right of the window, I can't help imagining what it must have been like for Pitt's mother when she was locked away for all those years. Did she feel like she'd been exiled from reality? Did she hold out any hope of rescue, or did this nightmare become her world? Did she die with nothing but memories of the unbearable heat in her dusty prison, loneliness, and her son's cruelty lingering in her mind?

I cross to the mattress, eyes focusing on a mildewed cardboard box filled with threadbare stuffed animals and a china tea set laid out on the floorboards, as if waiting for someone to come visit. The realization that Pitt's mother must have played with these toys, reverting to a childlike state while she was treated worse than the law allows owners to treat their pets, makes my throat close up and my eyes sting.

A second later, I've spun and started toward the pile of boxes and plastic storage tubs on the opposite side of the attic, more determined to find those tapes than ever. I'm ashamed to live in a world where monsters roam free, slipping off the hook with help from lawyers who think only about how to win and keep winning, not whether or not they should.

Pitt never should have walked free. He should be rotting in prison. The tapes can't send him there— he's already been acquitted, and can't be retried for his mother's murder—but I can use them to make him suffer.

It's like Gabe said, we can't rewrite history, but we can tip the scales back in the other direction. Teaching Pitt a lesson won't bring his mother back, but it will make the world a more just place, and might even make Pitt think twice before he indulges the evil part of his nature again.

My footsteps are light on the boards—making only the softest thuds as I make my way over to the part of the attic Pitt reserves for storage. It's the dead of the night and I'm assuming Pitt is asleep, but there's a chance he could wake up, hear me moving around, and come investigate. I force myself to move slowly, and when I reach the boxes and lean down to open the first one, I am careful not to let the cardboard flaps do more than whisper as they brush against each other.

I open box after box, container after container, but discover nothing more damning than a box of old Tupperware, and a tub filled with faded plaid shirts. Meanwhile, the physical exertion, combined with the heat in the attic and the fact that I'm wearing long sleeves and pants in the middle of June, join forces to make my head spin. Within five minutes, I'm sweating like every drop of liquid in my body is determined to commit suicide through my pores, and the pulse in my temple is throbbing so hard it thumps against my skull like a hammer.

By the time I finally shift a long, narrow container of books and letters to reveal an old-fash-ioned fruitcake tin like the ones my grandma used to hold her sewing supplies, I'm so dizzy my vision is beginning to blur.

I've never passed out before, but I'm pretty sure I'm about to. I know I should start back across the attic—I need to get some air before I lose consciousness and ensure I'm caught—but instead I reach for the tin, prying it open with swollen, heat-drugged fingers.

Inside, I discover DVDs. Eight of them. Each with a year scrawled across the silver in black marker.

Just like that, I know. I know he's transferred the VHS tapes he mentioned to Gabe's father—the one's he thought might prove he was guilty if they were discovered—to DVD. I *know* it. I know Pitt wanted to protect the mementos of his mother's suffering the way serial killers protect their trophies. I know he's *that* monstrous, and I suddenly wish I hadn't shied away from Gabe's suggestion that Pitt's punishment should fit his crime.

I want to see Pitt locked away in a room like this one, miserable and isolated without anyone or anything to comfort him, trapped so far from the nearest house no one can hear him scream. I want to watch his face on a television monitor as he realizes he'll be meeting the same end as his mother, a slow, torturous, miserable, nightmarish end that will leave him broken in a corner, rocking and mumbling and playing with toys, anything to try to escape, even if it's only in his mind, even if only for a little while.

But there would be no escape for him. He doesn't deserve escape. He deserves worse than prison. He deserves to die, to be wiped off the face of the earth before he can contaminate it any further or hurt any more innocent people.

I pull the cloth bag Gabe gave me last night from my pants pocket and stuff the DVDs inside, already tasting Pitt's blood on my tongue, sincerely longing to see the man die, to take part in the torture and killing myself. If Pitt were standing in front of me right now, I would pull the trigger, jab the knife, pull the noose, and I wouldn't feel a moment of remorse.

I stumble back across the attic with tears streaming from my eyes to wet my mask, hating myself for not being more fucked up by the thoughts reeling through my mind than I already am. But no matter how loudly my head insists that answering violence with violence isn't the answer, something deep in the hollows of my bones screams for vengeance, for blood to wash this horrible house clean before I burn it to the ground.

I reach the window and hang my head outside, drawing in deep lungsful of air, but though the dizziness fades, my head doesn't get any clearer. I keep thinking about what must be on the DVDs, wondering if Gabe and I are going to see Mrs. Pitt crying, begging to be set free, or simply lying on that bare mattress all alone. I wonder if we'll see her playing with her toys, rocking her stuffed animals, and setting out a tea party for visitors who are never going to arrive.

I wonder if her death is captured somewhere on the last DVD, and the acid surging in my stomach pushes up my throat like a fist.

I'm seconds away from getting sick when Gabe appears beneath the attic window. Just laying eyes on him, knowing he's close, is enough to calm my stomach, and send a tremor of relief quaking through me. His face is covered by his mask and the moonlight isn't strong enough for me to see the look in his eyes, but the black bag in his right hand makes me think he's succeeded. When he holds the bag up and gives it a victorious shake, I'm sure of it.

I answer him by holding my bag out the window, smiling when he gives me a thumbs- up and motions for me to come out.

We did it. We found everything we came for. The realization makes me want to throw back my head and shout at the stars, but shouting will have to wait until we're safely away from this horrible place.

I hook the bag's strap around my wrist and turn, putting one leg through the window at a time and sliding out on my belly. There's a moment of pain as the wood digs into my chest and forearms, but then I shift my weight and slowly straighten my elbows until I'm hanging from the sill by my clenched fingers.

The heat and my mini-breakdown have taken their toll on my body. I know I won't be able to hold on for long, but before my arms have the chance to start trembling, Gabe's hands are on my ankles, guiding my feet back onto his shoulders. I find my footing and lock my legs, finding my balance before I let go of the sill and bend my knees. I jump forward off of Gabe's shoulders, but he catches me around the waist on the way down, softening my landing, making sure my feet hit the grass with a gentle thud.

He pulls me to him, hugging me tight before he turns and starts back across the lawn. I follow, and seconds later we're across the gravel road, moving through the shadows on the wooded side of the street. I hand over my bag and we part ways with a whisper to see each other soon and a swift kiss before he disappears into the woods and I hurry back to the van.

I slam inside barely a minute later, arms shaking as I start the vehicle and pull away from the railroad tracks, heading back to town a different way than I came. I rip the mask off as I drive, and wiggle out of the black shirt, revealing the green tank top beneath. The top is soaked through with sweat, but hopefully no one who sees me at the Laundromat will think anything of it, and I can always chock a sweaty shirt up to sleeping without the air conditioning running.

Ten minutes later I have my alibi—I check the dryer where I deliberately left the clothes earlier today, making sure my sigh of relief is performed facing the security cameras—and I'm back on the road, heading for home. I park the van and slip in through the back door, relieved to find the house as relatively quiet as when I left it. I hear Sean snoring in his room, the hum of the box fans whirring in bedroom windows, and the whine of the fridge as it struggles to keep the milk cool, but nothing that would indicate anyone woke up while I was gone.

I snag the note I left for Danny and head upstairs, stripping off clothes as I head for the shower, wanting to be clean when Gabe arrives at my window. Clean and wearing nothing but a bed sheet and a smile.

We've finished the job. Now, it's time to celebrate.

CHAPTER 20

GABE

It is my soul that calls upon my name;
How silver-sweet sound lovers' tongues by night, -
Shakespeare

"I've been waiting for almost an hour."

Her voice drifts to me as I climb through her window. I turn to find her framed in a crooked rectangle of moonlight on her double bed, wearing nothing but a white cotton sheet draped across her middle. It covers her breasts and reaches down far enough to conceal her thatch of tight blond curls and those sweet inches between her legs I can't wait to get my hands on…my mouth on…my cock in, buried balls deep.

"What took you so long?" she asks.

"I made sure the DVDs were what we thought they were," I say, eyes tracking up and down her body. "Then I hid them. I didn't want you to have to watch."

"Thanks. I don't think I could have."

"You're welcome," I murmur. "You look…comfortable."

"Not really." She lifts her arms over her head as she stretches, wrists crossed. Moonlight caresses her pale skin, while shadows darken the hollows of her armpits.

I want to kiss her there, taste the tang and salt of her sweat. I want to kiss her ribs, the curve of her hip, the bends in her knees. I want to press my lips to her anklebone and rake my teeth over each one of her toes. I want to fist my hand in her hair and hold her so close, kiss her so deeply, that we disappear into each other.

I need her so much I feel like I'm going to disintegrate into a pile of lustful ash if I don't touch her soon, but I force myself to stand still, memorizing this moment, etching each detail into my brain.

This is a memory I want to keep for the rest of my life. This is one of the pictures I want to flash before my eyes when I'm fighting for my final breath.

She's so beautiful, like something out of one of my dreams, the dreams that are always about her. Always. Ever since the night I first kissed her addictive lips.

"Are you just going to stand there?" she asks, thighs shifting lazily, shushing against the sheet, the feline way she moves making my already swollen cock strain the front of my pants. "Or are you going to come help me out?"

"Depends." I step out of my shoes, setting my keys and wallet on the desk near the window, but keeping my eyes on her. "What do you need help with?"

"I went out with this guy tonight," she says, one hand sliding across her pillow, down until her fingertips brush the side of her face. "And the date was really good, and really…bad."

"How's that?" I take a step forward, gaze glued to her hand, the one sliding down her neck, across her chest to disappear beneath the sheet.

"Well…the good part is that we gave a horrible person a little of what's coming to him," she says, sheet shifting as her hand moves beneath it. "The bad part is that I had to come home alone…" She holds my gaze, a challenge in her eyes as her hand moves lower. "I've been sitting her thinking about the man I went out with, and how much I want him to touch me. But he took forever to get here, and now I'm so wet it's embarrassing."

"Show me." My hands fist at my sides. I fight to maintain control, to draw out this moment of anticipation a little longer before I join her on the bed and show her how sorry I am for making her wait.

"Show you? Like this?" She fists the sheet in her free hand, drawing it up her body until her pussy— and the slim fingers sliding up and down her slick flesh, teasing in and out of her swollen folds—are bare to me.

"Like that," I say, throat tight, balls tighter. "Spread your legs wider. I want to see every inch."

She spreads her legs, but it's still not wide enough.

"Wider." My breath comes faster as she obeys. "Now reach down and spread your lips."

Again she obeys, reaching down and opening her sex to me in a way I know some people would find obscene, but that makes me so hot it feels like my head is going to explode. Seeing her like this— so turned on and vulnerable, ready and willing to give herself to me—makes me want to consume her, to devour her pussy with my mouth until she comes, screaming my name, bathing my face in more of her heat before I rise up and push inside her. I can't wait to fuck her with all the need that's been building inside of me, like tension along a fault line, until it feels like my bones are going to shatter if I don't relieve the pressure.

But not yet, not just yet…

"Finger yourself," I say. "Just one finger."

She follows my instructions, the way Caitlin does in situations like this. She gives me shit outside the bedroom any time she pleases, but when it's time for our clothes to come off, she hands me the reins. It's one of the things I adore about her, one of the many things that have conspired to make any minute without Caitlin in it seem like a waste of precious time.

I watch her slender finger dip in and out of her slick entry. She's so wet her sex glistens in the moonlight, beckoning me to come and taste, to consume and be consumed, by the only girl who has ever made me feel like every tightly locked door inside of me is being thrown open, all at once. There's quickly becoming nowhere to hide from the intense, insane, impossible things she makes me feel, but I'm starting not to care. This thing with Caitlin feels…inevitable, like I was meant to spend this last summer with her, like I was meant to rip my heart out of my chest and hand it over to this girl.

Still beating.

Still raw and ugly and messy, but real, the realest thing I've ever known.

"Does that feel good?" I ask. "Is one finger enough?"

She shakes her head, chest rising and falling faster as she increases her pace.

"What about two?" I strip my shirt over my head and toss it to the ground without breaking eye contact. "Will two get you off?"

"No." She shakes her head again, moaning softly as she watches me undo my belt. "God, Gabe. Please…"

"Please, what?" I pull a condom from my back pocket and toss it on the foot of the bed before flipping open the buttons on my fly and shoving my jeans down. I step free of them and toe off my socks before making quick work of my black boxer briefs.

The hunger in Caitlin's expression as the briefs vanish and my engorged cock falls free, bobbing heavily between my thighs, is almost enough to make me come. I swear I can feel that look like she just fisted me in her hand and I'm on fire. My skin is hot and feverish and my eyes are burning and my blood is lava coursing through my veins, determined to scorch every cell in my body to pieces if I don't cool off.

And then, without memory of moving, I'm on top of her and her skin is cool and her hair is cooler and still a bit damp and she smells so perfectly like Caitlin—like night flowers and spice and treasures hidden in cedar boxes—that something inside of me takes flight. I'm suddenly flying, soaring miles above the ground, beyond the reach of the ordinary world and all its petty concerns and everyday tragedies.

I am above it all, and Caitlin is right there with me.

Our lips meet in a bruising kiss and her tongue spears into my mouth and her taste floods through me. Her legs wrap around my hips and pull me closer, close enough for me to feel the wet core of her against my stomach and realize shifting up a few inches would put me inside her. I shift the other way, instead, kissing my way down her throat, where her pulse beats the same frantic rhythm as my own. I press kisses to her shoulder—one for each perfect freckle—before moving lower and taking her nipple in my mouth.

I want to wait, I want to kiss her sinfully soft breast, trace the place beneath, where breast meets ribs with my tongue, torment her until she begs, but

I don't have the control. Not tonight, when we've done what we've done, and she was so perfect, like she was born to do these wicked, wonderful things with me.

All these wonderful things, and what's happening here in this bed the most wonderful of all.

"Gabe." She fists her hands in my hair, pulling me closer to her breast as I tease her taut nipple between my tongue and the roof of my mouth, trapping her there, holding her captive until she groans and her nails dig into my scalp hard enough to sting.

"Gentle," I whisper against her hot flesh before transferring my attention to her other breast, but I don't really want her to be gentle.

I want to drive her crazy. I want her feral with lust for me. I want to feel her nails breaking my skin and her teeth digging into my bicep as I slam inside her.

I flick my tongue across her right nipple, while capturing the recently abandoned left nipple in my hand, rolling it between my finger and thumb. I'm so hard my cock pulses with an angry heartbeat of its own, but I force myself to wait. I wait until she's writhing beneath me, until her nails are raking down my back and her hips are bucking into my ribs and she's cussing me in a frantic, breathy voice that is so fucking sexy I'm pretty sure I could come just by listening to her, but I don't want to come anywhere but in her pussy, that sweet, slick, hot pussy that I know is going to be the best place I've ever been.

"Fuck, Gabe," she says, with a moan that becomes a whimper of pain. "Please! Fucking please, you piece of shit."

I smile against her breast before I trap her nipple and bite down hard enough to make her yip. "You want me to fuck you?" I ask, surging back over her slim form, crushing her mouth with a kiss before she can answer.

"Fuck yes," she says, fighting to get the words out as we kiss hard enough for me to feel her teeth through our lips. "Yes!"

I reach down to the foot of the bed, ripping open the condom and sheathing myself in seconds, and then I'm on top of her again, her soft skin hot against mine, her arms tangling around my neck and her legs locking around my waist as I position myself and drive inside her with one fierce thrust.

She is even hotter and tighter than I'd imagined she'd be, like a fist gripping my cock so tight I see black stars bursting at the edge of my vision.

She cries out—a sound that is more pain than pleasure—and stiffens against me. I feel her thigh muscles clench on either side of mine, and still inside her, forcing myself to resist the urge to start pumping, realizing too late that Caitlin is even more of a contradiction than I'd assumed.

"Shit," I curse, biting my lip as I trap her head between my hands and stare down into her eyes, not surprised to see the lust from a moment before replaced by a furrowed brow and lips pressed tight together. "Why didn't you tell me?"

"Tell you what?" she asks, her voice strung as tight as the rest of her.

"That you were a virgin."

"I told you I don't date," she says, wincing. "I thought you knew."

"How the fuck would I know, Caitlin?" I ask, anger at myself for hurting her creeping into my tone. "Virgins don't act the way you act. Virgins don't finger themselves in your car when you tell them to, or carry on a fucking conversation while you're staring at their pussy, or—"

"So what? I'm supposed to act shy and awkward and ashamed of my body? Just because other girls do?" she asks, eyes flashing. "Well, sorry, but I'm not like that. And I'm only a virgin because I've never had the time to get around to getting rid of it."

"You make your virginity sound like an old couch."

"Well, yeah, it means about that much to me," she snaps, shoving at my chest. "But I'm sorry fucking a virgin is such a pain in your ass."

"It's not a—"

"Get off me," she says, shoving harder.

"Wait." I trap her wrists in my hands, pressing her arms into the mattress above her head before adding in a softer voice, "You're not a pain in my ass. I didn't mean to upset you."

Caitlin's breath shudders out. "Well, you did. You made me feel like an idiot."

"I'm sorry," I say. "I'm just…I didn't want to hurt you. If I'd known, I would have taken things more slowly. I don't…I don't ever want to hurt you."

The frown remains on her face, but the tension slowly leaks out of her arms. "You didn't hurt me."

"Liar," I say, pressing a kiss to her cheek.

"Okay, it hurt at first, but now…it's not so bad."

"Not so bad isn't the way I want you to remember our first time." I kiss her other cheek and the tip of her nose before bringing my lips to hers.

I part her lips, apologizing with every deep, deliberate stroke of my tongue against hers, knowing there are better ways to make up than with words. I kiss her until her breath comes faster and her tongue swirls hungrily through my mouth and my softening erection surges back to life. But I don't begin to move. I stay buried and still inside her, kissing her until she squirms her wrists free and brings her hands back to my shoulders, pulling me closer as her fingers thread into my hair. I kiss her until her thighs finally begin to relax and only then do I bring my hand back to her breast, kneading the soft flesh before brushing my thumbs across her nipple.

She sighs into my mouth and arches her back. I follow her cue and intensify my attention, teasing and rolling and pinching first one nipple and then the other, until her hips begin to roll in little circles and I reach down, cupping one ass cheek in each hand, shifting the angle of penetration until my pubic bone presses against her clit.

Her gasp as her next hip circle provides friction confirms we've found the sweet spot. I circle my hips, nudging at her clit with thrusts so shallow my cock barely moves inside her tight, slick sheath. My balls ache and my stomach clenches with the need to pull back and drive inside her, again and again until I explode, but this isn't about me. Not yet, not until Caitlin comes.

I drop my lips to her breast, pulling her nipple into the warmth of my mouth, flicking my tongue across her tip as I continue to rock gently against her and her breath comes faster and her fingers dig into my bare shoulders.

"God, Gabe," she pants, back arching, legs spreading wider, meeting each of my thrusts with increasingly desperate thrusts of her own. "God…I can't…this feels…."

"Good?" I smother her response with another kiss, blood pulsing faster as she moans into my mouth and reaches down, digging her nails into my ass.

"So good, so good," she chants, breath puffing against my wet lips. "God, Gabe, God…I think I'm… I think…"

"Come for me, baby," I say, fighting for control as our tempo grows more frantic and I feel her inner walls tightening around me. "God, I want to feel you come on my cock, Caitlin."

"Yes," she says. "Yes!"

She cries out, a sound I echo as her pussy grips me tight, her orgasm rippling through her with sharp waves I can feel massaging the aching length of me until my vision blurs and every bit of blood in my body surges to the eight inches buried inside her and there is no more holding back, no more control.

I pull out to the end of her and surge back in, thrusting in and out of her sweet pussy that is so wet and hot and tight and perfect. Perfect. Like her, like the way she fits against me, like the way she makes me feel like there is finally someone in the world who understands.

And then her hands are on my face and she's pulling me down for another kiss as she wraps her legs around my hips, pulling me deeper with every thrust. I pump into her, faster, faster, until there is nothing but the sound of our hungry bodies pounding against each other and our moans and sighs as we kiss and lick and bite, fighting our way toward the end of this, the moment when there will be nothing but pleasure, nothing but her and me and God…

God….

I call her name as I come, my orgasm rocketing through me until I can't breathe, can't see, can't think of anything but this bliss. It's so good, like this, with her, so much better than it's ever been before. I am broken and made whole; I am shattered to pieces and put back together with her kiss. I need her, crave her, want to keep her here in this bed with me forever. This is more than a way to forget, so much more.

And I am so very fucking screwed.

By the time I collapse on top of her, catching my breath as my cock twitches with aftershocks of pleasure, I know I've made a horrible mistake. I curse, smothering the sound in the crook of Caitlin's neck as her fingers drift up and down my sweat soaked back, hating myself. Hating how weak and pathetic and soft I am, soft as any dumb kid with his first crush when I thought I was so hard no one could ever crack the shell around my heart.

I hadn't even been sure I had a heart, at least not the way other people did. I thought I would always be on the outside of that type of emotion, too warped around the edges to fit with someone as perfectly as Caitlin and I fit.

It's horrible. And wonderful. And pointless, and suddenly I feel trapped in this room, smothered by the tender way she touches me.

I have to get out. I have to be alone, find some-place where I can think.

"Don't," she says, holding me to her when I try to pull away. "Stay."

"I can't," I say, throat so tight I can barely force out the words. "I told you at the beginning of this— I'm leaving at the end of the summer, even if I am your first. I just…I can't. I won't. This is going to end in two and a half months, no matter what happens."

She cups my face, urging me from her neck. I allow her to move me, but keep my gaze on the blank wall behind her head. I can feel her looking up at me, but I don't look down. I can't look her in the eye, not yet.

"Gabe," she says, a smile in her voice. "Gabe look at me."

I don't, not until she laughs beneath her breath.

"What's so funny?" I glance down to find her smiling up at me.

"Nothing," she says, with a gentle shake of her head. "I just…you don't have to worry. I told you, I wasn't holding on to my virginity like some prize possession. I wasn't saving it for someone special. It didn't mean anything to me."

I scowl. Her words are exactly what I want to hear. So why do they hurt? Why do they make me want to storm out of here even more than I did before?

"I love what we just did," she says, cooling the anger building inside of me. "And I feel really close to you—now, and even before, when we were planning everything together, but…" She strokes a hand down my face, her touch calming and exciting at the same time. "But I don't want anything more than the summer, either. I have too much going on in my life to get swept up in some big relationship…thing. I'm not going to make any demands. There won't be any tears when we say goodbye."

She pauses, drawing in a breath as her fingertips trail across my ribs and around to my back, making me very aware that I'm still buried inside her and not feeling near as spent as I did a minute ago. "I just…I love this," she continues. "I love spending time with you, and I have never felt more alive than I did tonight. I don't want to give that up, and I don't want you to feel like you have to run away because I'm falling for you."

"You're not?" I ask, holding her gaze, keeping my expression neutral.

"No," she says, smiling again. "But I would really like to do this again. Soon. Like…really soon."

My lips curve despite myself. "You're not in pain?"

"A little, but…" She lifts a bare shoulder as her gaze falls to my chest. "But I kind of like it. It makes it feel more…real, if that makes any sense."

"It does." Everything she says makes sense to me, *she* makes sense to me in a way no one else ever has.

She may not be falling, but I am.

Falling, falling, fallen.

I've never been in love before, but I'm pretty sure this is what it feels like, at least for me. Like I'm drowning and never want to come up for air, like I live for her sweet, sexy smile. Like I would walk to the ends of the earth for just one more kiss, and I would rip apart anyone who dared to hurt her with my bare hands.

I was worried *I* might hurt her—that she was getting as swept up in all this as I am—but she's made of tougher stuff. Her head is still on straight and her eyes wide open. She'll be fine, and I don't really matter, not the way she does.

So maybe it's okay for me to love her, to cup this

secret fire in my hands and see how big it can grow before it's snuffed out at the summer's end.

"What are you thinking?" she asks.

That I love you. That I'd do anything for you.

Aloud, I say. "Let me get rid of this, and I'll show you."

I dispose of the condom and return to the bed and in moments we're tangled up in each other all over again. It's slower this time, sweeter. We take our time, lingering over each kiss, each rush of breath over sweat-slicked skin, and by the time I push inside her a second time I am even more lost than I was before.

For the first time, I understand what it feels like to make love. Not fuck, not screw, not have sex. I make love to Caitlin, am destroyed and reborn in her arms, and I fall asleep barely noticing the dull ache at the base of my skull.

The ache that warns that there is no pleasure without pain, no love without hate, and no happiness without sacrifice.

CHAPTER 21

CAITLIN

Five Weeks Later...

May you have the hindsight to know
where you've been,
the foresight to know where you are going,
and the insight to know when you have gone too far. -
Irish proverb

*T*race around the side of the squat, concrete building, boots pounding against the asphalt as I sprint toward where Gabe leans against the chain link fence surrounding the storage facility. I push hard with everything in me, heart slamming against my ribs as I fight to put distance between me and the nasty surprise that was waiting for me in locker seventy-three.

"Get back here!" The man's shout comes from behind me, but not far behind.

Not near far enough.

I push harder, arms pumping up and down like pistons, becoming flashes of black that blur at the edges of my vision.

"That's my fucking money!" the man shouts. "Stop, you piece of shit!"

I reach Gabe, grabbing a handful of his black shirt as I round the corner, dragging him along with me. "Run!" I gasp when he trips and nearly falls.

I'm so out of breath I can barely form the word, but my lookout seems like he's in worse shape. Gabe rights himself and stumbles toward the sidewalk, unsteady on his feet. Not skipping a beat, I hook my arm through his and pull him along beside me, past the entrance to another, low-rent storage facility, a shuttered bail bondsman's shop, and on toward the residential part of this faded Charleston neighborhood.

I wonder what's wrong with him, but there's no time to ask. The man who caught me breaking into his storage unit is nearing fifty, but he's in good shape. A hell of a lot better shape than you'd expect a man to be in after spending twelve years in prison.

Of course, according to the Federal Bureau of Prison's Inmate Locator, Grant Harrison is *still* in prison, so...

"Give me back my money!" the very *not*-still-in-prison Harrison shouts. His footsteps slap the pavement behind me as he barrels down the middle of the deserted road, shouting that he was robbed, setting dogs to barking behind the rickety fence of a house on my left and my heart leaping up to lodge in my throat.

I haul Gabe alongside me as I run, cutting down a dark side street before emerging on another main road. My lungs feel like they're full of acid and a cramp knifes into my side, but just when I'm sure I can't keep going with Gabe leaning even a third of his weight on my shoulders, he seems to recover.

He stands up straight and picks up his pace, pulling ahead as we cut through the backyard of an abandoned house and sprint toward the sagging shed where we parked the van. By the time I slam into the passenger's side, Gabe has the engine running and his foot on the pedal.

He roars out of the shed, tires squealing as he shifts from reverse to drive and peals down Pinewood Place, headed toward the highway.

"He's not there. He didn't see us pull out," I pant as I turn to look out the rear glass, making sure Harrison isn't going to be able to identify the make and model of the van.

"Fuck," Gabe curses.

"And I got the money," I add, ripping off my mask. "We're good. We're fine."

"We're not fine." Gabe yanks his mask off, tossing it to the floor at my feet as he takes a right on Ferncrest, then an immediate left, following the escape route we planned in advance. "Harrison is supposed to be in prison. How the fuck did he catch you breaking in?"

I shake my head, still catching my breath as I

turn back around and reach for my seatbelt with trembling hands. "I don't know, but he's obviously out, and sleeping in that storage unit. He woke up while I was going through the trunk."

Gabe curses again.

"Yeah. I about peed my pants when he started yelling. Scared me half to death." I clutch the bag of money in my lap, drawing strength from the hard lumps inside. It's full of tightly rolled one hundred dollar bills, at least thirty or forty thousand dollars, earned by the abuse of Grant Harrison's daughter, Cathy, when she was a little girl.

Back in the early two thousands, Harrison made kiddie porn featuring his underage daughter and sold it on an underground website, making a mint before he was caught. All of his assets were seized by the federal government, but his daughter insisted there was more money, that her father had hidden it away somewhere. Cathy hired Gabe's dad to sue her father, but overdosed before the case could go to trial, losing a lifelong battle with drugs and addiction that started when she was ten years old, when her father used to roll her a joint to help her relax before he filmed her.

Gabe and I read Cathy Harrison's file yesterday, and only spent a few hours last night researching the job. The file said that Grant's sister, Marjorie, had leased a storage unit shortly before Grant was convicted. Gabe and I did some digging and learned Marjorie had moved to Florida, but that the storage unit was still in her name and paid up for the next four years. We googled Grant to verify he was still in federal prison, did a drive-by of the storage facility to make sure they didn't have anyone on duty at night, and swung into Charleston to acquire industrial strength bolt cutters for the lock on the fence before calling our preparation finished.

Since that night at Pitt's, Gabe and I have hit two private residences, a nursing home, and a medical practice, all without a single hitch. We secured Pitt's resignation with a blackmail note—ensuring Danny was passed into the eighth grade—did our part to avenge the innocent people hurt by an embezzler, an identity thief, a crooked doctor, and a serial rapist, and have made ourselves a hundred thousand dollars richer in the process.

A hundred, fucking, thousand dollars. After tonight, we'll be close to one hundred and forty. It's mind-boggling, more money than I would have earned in *four years* working my job at the diner, and it's been so easy.

Maybe too easy. And maybe Gabe and I are getting careless.

"Do you think he got out of prison today?" I ask, breath finally returning to normal. "I mean, I guess that's possible."

"It's more likely there's another Grant Harrison in federal lock up," Gabe says, turning onto the highway, heading back toward home. "We should have made sure the one in Edgefield was ours before we hit the storage unit. And *I* should have been the one to go in, while you kept lookout. You can practice your lock picking when your life isn't in danger."

"There was no way we could have known anyone was in there," I say. "And I got away. I'm faster than I was even a few weeks ago."

"You're not faster than a bullet," Gabe says, sounding grouchier than I've ever heard him. "What if Harrison had had a gun?"

My brow furrows. "You weren't worried about that when we robbed the pawnshop."

"Things are different now," Gabe says softly. "We're different."

I'm silent for a moment, refusing to acknowledge the way his words make my heart do a giddy flip in my chest. We *are* different now. Back then, I wasn't even sure I liked Gabe; now, I can't imagine my life without him in it. Now, I want to spend every waking minute with him, and go to sleep next to him every night.

Now, I am completely screwed, because even if Gabe loves me the way I think he does, I know he's serious about this only being for the summer. If he finds out I want more, he'll leave. He'll leave and I don't know what I'll do. I don't know if I'll be able to hold it together all alone now that I know what it feels like to have a partner, someone who makes me feel beautiful and fascinating. Someone who gets every part of me, even the parts that aren't polished, or pretty, and don't like to play by the rules.

"I think it's time to take a break," he says, his tone as deflated as I'm feeling.

A break doesn't mean the end, but there's something in his voice, something that makes my heart feel bruised.

"Okay," I say, forcing an upbeat note into the word that I don't feel. "Slowing down isn't always a bad thing."

Which reminds me…

"Are you okay?" I turn to face him, studying his profile in the shifting yellow light of the headlights streaming down the other side of the highway. "What was up back there? Did you feel sick, or something?"

"I don't know," Gabe says, eyes focused on the road ahead. "I felt all right, but when I tried to run…" He shrugs. "I don't know. I'm fine now. I must have gotten overheated standing there sweating my balls off in long sleeves. It's fucking hot as hell tonight."

"Does that mean you're not going to sleep over at the Cooney sweat lodge?" I ask, brushing away a brown curl that's stuck to his forehead.

A smile flickers on his lips but it's gone by the time the next pair of headlights sweep across his face. "Not tonight. My parents saw me go up to bed. If I don't come back down again tomorrow morning, they might notice. The Alexanders occasionally notice each other on Sundays, and they're my alibi so…"

"Okay," I say, ignoring the disappointment that flashes in my chest. "But I'll see you tomorrow for dinner?"

"Wouldn't miss it," he says, passing a battered pickup truck going fifty in the fast lane.

Sunday night burger night in the backyard has become a tradition. The kids look forward to it every week, and so do I. I love seeing Gabe relaxed and happy, playing soccer with the boys, or giving Emmie a ride on his shoulders so she can peek over the fence at our crazy cat lady neighbor's new kittens. He's so good with the kids. It makes me wish…

I press my lips together and stare out the window at the dark woods flashing by, banishing the thought before it can find its tail end. It doesn't matter what I wish. This is only for the summer, and it will be over before I can blink.

We don't talk much more on the way home, and Gabe doesn't even try to sneak a peek as I change out of my blacks and into the clothes I was wearing when I left the house. The air in the van is quiet, thick with tension, like the air before a storm, and all too soon Gabe is pulling up in front of my house.

At one in the morning, every window is dark, except for a blue light flickering behind the living room curtains, making me think Isaac must have fallen asleep in front of the television. I told him I was going dancing with Sherry—which I did, for an hour, before I left her flirting with her favorite bartender and slipped out of the club to meet up with Gabe.

I know I should feel bad for lying to one of my best friends, but I don't. I don't feel bad about much these days, not lying, or stealing, or any of the other things Gabe and I do on a regular basis. Maybe that means my moral compass is more messed up than I could have imagined before I met Gabe, but I'm still there for the kids when they need me, my stomach is calmer than it's been since I was a kid, and I'm happy in a brand new way.

This isn't the "stolen moment" kind of happiness I knew before—snatched between the teeth of one crisis and the next—it's something that starts deep inside of me and spreads out to envelope every aspect of my life. It's a seed that was planted and nurtured by this summer with Gabe, and a part of me is terrified that my happiness will wither and die when he leaves in the fall.

But even terror can't cut as deep when Gabe is sitting next to me.

I lean over to kiss him goodbye, and it is sexy and honest and intense—the way kissing him always is—but he tastes sadder than usual, salty, like a tear.

"Are you sure you're okay?" I ask after we pull away, running a gentle hand down his face. "Is everything all right?"

He holds my gaze for a beat before smiling a smile that doesn't reach his eyes. "Everything's fine. I'll see you tomorrow."

"See you tomorrow," I echo as Gabe claims the bag of money from the floorboards and we slip out of the van, going our separate ways. He starts down the driveway, headed back to where he parked the Beamer a few blocks over, turning to blow me a kiss at the end of the drive. I lift my hand and wave, swallowing all the words that want to come out—like *don't go,* and *I'll miss you*, and *I love you*.

I love him. I *love* him and it is wonderful and horrible and it…is what it is. There's no changing it, no matter how much it hurts to think of saying goodbye.

But I'm too tired to think any more tonight.

I slip inside the front door, closing it as quietly as I can behind me, expecting to find Isaac passed out and drooling on the couch, but when I turn, he's sitting up, staring at me with an intensity that makes anxiety skitter across my skin.

He jabs mute on the T.V. remote, and my gut twists, the instinctive feeling that I've screwed up hitting before my mind can sort out what I could have done wrong.

"Is everything okay?" I ask, hanging my boho bag on one of the wall hooks inside the door. "Are the kids all right?"

"The kids are fine." Isaac tosses the remote onto the couch cushions before knotting his thick arms across his chest. "But I'm not sure I can say the same about you."

I frown as I run a hand through my still sweat-damp hair. "What's that supposed to mean? I thought you said it was okay if I stayed out. If you wanted me home earlier, you should have just—"

"This isn't about staying out," Isaac says. "Your

dad came by earlier, right when I was cleaning up dinner."

I curse beneath my breath as I kick off my shoes and shuffle over to the couch, suddenly even more exhausted than I was before. "I'm sorry." I collapse next to Isaac with a sigh. "You should have called me. I would have come home and handled it."

Isaac shifts, staring down at me as I lean back, resting my head on the lumpy cushions. "He wasn't drunk, Caitlin. He was as sober as I've ever seen him, and really fucking upset."

I pull my knees up, hugging them to my chest. "What about?"

"What do you think?" Isaac asks, sympathetic gaze drilling into mine. But this time I have the feeling I'm not the one he's feeling sorry for. "He's a wreck about the law suit, C. He can't believe you're really going to take the kids away."

I grunt. "Can't believe I'm going to get the state to garnish his VA check for child support is more like it."

"It's not like that." Isaac shakes his head. "Chuck said he'll sign the house and part of his check over to you and give you full legal guardianship of the kids. He just doesn't want to go to court and lose his parental rights. He knows the kids are the only good things he ever did with his life. It's killing him to think of losing them."

I hug my knees tighter, and my jaw clenches.

"Just call off the suit," Isaac continues when I don't respond. "He'll give you everything you want.

You'll get the stability you need for the kids, he'll still be their dad on paper, you'll save a bunch of stress not going to court... Everybody wins."

"If he cares so much about the kids, how come it took a lawsuit to make him do the right thing?" I ask. "And why should I feel sorry for a man who has done nothing but make my life harder from the moment I was born?"

I drop my feet to the ground, bracing my elbows on my knees and squeezing my hands together in a single fist. "I'm glad he feels like shit. It's time he had a taste of what it feels like to be helpless and scared."

"Come on, Cait. This isn't like you. You don't take pleasure in other people's pain, even your dad's." Isaac puts a hand on my shoulder, squeezing softly, but his touch doesn't calm me the way it usually does.

I shrug his hand off, and stand, pacing a few steps away from the couch. "I'm sorry I'm disappointing you, but this is how I feel. I don't care if Chuck is losing his shit. I'm going through with the suit. For the kids."

"You're going through with it to get revenge," Isaac says, looking at me like I'm a stranger who wandered into the living room. "You're different, C. Ever since you started going out with Gabe. It's like he's brought out this...fierce, scary side of you, or something."

I roll my eyes, not liking how close Isaac is getting to the truth. "Gabe has nothing to do with this. He was nice enough to ask his dad to represent the case for free. That's it. I'm making decisions on my own." I cross my arms, shrugging as I drop my eyes to the threadbare carpet. "Besides, I don't think there's anything wrong with being fierce. Sometimes you need to be fierce to get the job done."

"Fierce, but not cruel." Isaac stands, stepping closer until he's looming over me. "There's a difference and you know it."

I shrug again, but the movement is smaller, less confident.

Maybe Isaac is right; maybe I am being cruel.

If Chuck agrees to give me everything I'd get from going to court—except for parental custody—then what do I have to gain from going through with the suit? As legal guardian, I'd have the power to make decisions for the kids, and if the house is in my name, I can call the police and have Chuck carted off if he refuses to leave when I tell him to.

And maybe, if I meet him in the middle, Chuck will remember I did him a solid. Maybe he'll stay sober more often, and start coming around to spend time with the family, instead of stumbling in drunk, asking for money, and leaving as soon as he gets what he wants.

"And maybe pigs are going to fly," I mumble to the carpet.

Isaac sighs. "I know you aren't talking to me, but I understand what you're feeling. It's hard to believe that people can change, but it can happen."

No it can't. People don't change. Looking

through Gabe's father's files has made that clear. People may alter their behavior or evolve in other ways as they age, but folks who are rotten at their cores, stay rotten.

My father is one of the rotten ones, I know that, no matter how much a naïve part of me wants to believe that it's the alcohol talking every time Chuck calls me a bitch or backhands Danny. The alcohol may fuel the fire, but the damp wood that's burning and stinking up everything, is all Chuck. And I'm done with Chuck. I don't have any more empathy left for him, or anyone like him.

I look up, meeting Isaac's gentle gaze with a hard one. "My mind's made up. I'm going through with the suit, and I'm going to make sure Chuck has as little authorized contact with the kids as possible. It's what's best for them."

"It's best for them to never see their dad again?" Isaac asks. "I mean, I know he's a shit sometimes, but tonight he was great. You should have seen how excited Sean was to see him. That little boy still loves his dad, and wants him in his life."

"He'll get over it," I say, voice cold. "The rest of us have."

Isaac stares at me, into me, like he's waiting for me to break and confess I was just kidding. But I'm not kidding. I'm not the same weak, one-step-away-from-disaster girl Isaac's known since we were kids. I'm in control now. I have the power, and I'm not giving it up without a fight.

"Fine," he says, shaking his head as he steps back.

"But for what it's worth, I think you're making a mistake."

"Noted. Thanks for watching the kids tonight," I say tightly, eager to see Isaac walking out my door for the first time in my life.

"Yeah, well…I love them." Isaac props his hands on his hips, glancing down at his feet before meeting my eyes. "I love you, too. I will always love you, but that doesn't mean I have to love the way you're acting since you started dating Gabe."

I sigh. "I need to get to bed, Isaac. I'm tired."

"He's bad for you, Caitlin," Isaac says, stubbornly. "One day you're going to wake up and realize just how bad. I just hope it's not too late."

"Too late for what?" I ask, temper flaring. "To go back to being everyone's willing little doormat? Because that's not going to happen, and if that's the only version of me you can accept, maybe we shouldn't hang out so much anymore."

"We haven't hung out in weeks." Isaac's voice is as hot as mine. "You're too busy for your friends anymore. All you care about is him."

"So you're jealous, is that it?" I snap before I think about what I'm saying.

Isaac blinks, but after a moment, the anger vanishes from his eyes, leaving behind a naked, vulnerable look. "Maybe I am. Maybe I thought…"

I dig my fingers into my upper arms, heart beating faster, shocked and scared and wishing I could rewind time to three minutes ago and run up to bed. I don't want him to finish his sentence; I silently pray for him to stop talking and walk out the door, but God isn't answering my prayers tonight any more than He ever has.

"I thought it would be me," Isaac says, voice thick, rough. "I thought that if you ever decided to make time for someone in that way…it would be me."

"What about Heather?" I ask, pulse racing in my throat. "You have a girlfriend, Isaac, I never—"

"I'm with Heather because I couldn't be with you," he says, making my stomach lurch. "I knew how bad your mom and sister running off fucked you up, and I didn't think you'd ever let someone into your life in that way. But if I'd thought…if I'd even had a little hope that you—"

"Don't." I back a step away, shaking my head fast. "I don't want to hear it. Just… Let's pretend this never happened. Just go, and we'll pretend—"

"I'm tired of pretending," Isaac says. "And Heather's tired, too. She knows I'm in love with you. We fought about it that first night you went out with Gabe. Things haven't been right between us since. She's going to break up with me, sooner or later, but I'm not going to wait around for it to happen anymore. I'm breaking up with her. Tomorrow. I can't keep lying to her, or myself."

I shake my head again. "I…I don't know what to say."

"Say you'll think about making a different choice," Isaac says, hope in his voice that makes me want to stab myself in the ears so I don't have to hear it, don't have to realize how stupid I've been, or how much I'm going to have to hurt someone I care about.

"I can't," I whisper, pressing my lips together. "I'm sorry, Isaac, I don't… I don't love you that way."

Isaac's brow furrows, but the longing doesn't leave his expression. "Yeah, not now, I know that. But…take some time. Think about all we've been through, all we mean to each other. There's more to what we have than friendship, and I know there have been times when you've felt it, too."

I force myself to meet his eyes, knowing he won't believe me unless he sees the truth in my face. "No, I haven't. I'm in love with Gabe, and I don't want to be with anyone else. Not now. Maybe…not ever."

"Never is a long time." Isaac's eyes begin to shine. "He's going to leave you, Caitlin. He's not the kind of guy who sticks around."

"I know that," I say. "It doesn't matter. It doesn't change the way I feel." I pull in a breath, my ribs aching as they expand. "I'm sorry, Isaac. I really am."

He sniffs, swiping the back of his hand across his mouth before he smiles. "Yeah, well, I hope I'm wrong. I hope he doesn't break your heart. But if he does… I can't be the shoulder you cry on anymore."

"Okay," I whisper, hating the misery that twists Isaac's face as he backs toward the door.

"Great, well…" He grabs his keys from one of the wall hooks. "Good luck with everything. I'll see you when I see you."

I open my mouth to say something to make this better, but I can't think of a damned thing. I watch him go, and then stand in the middle of the living room alone for a good five minutes. I stand and watch the twisted blue shadows flickering in the corners of the ceiling, feeling like the world has turned upside down.

CHAPTER 22

GABE

Cut off even in the blossoms of my sin...
No reckoning made, but sent to my account with all my
imperfections on my head.
-Shakespeare

Sunday morning dawns with numbness in my right arm.

I think I must have slept on it wrong, but then I roll over and the horizon line outside the window goes crooked, shifting back and forth the way it did last night when I was trying to run from the storage facility. I close my eyes and open them, close and open, but the world refuses to steady and soon my stomach is pitching right along with the field of hay behind Darby Hill.

I close my eyes and force myself to go back to sleep, not wanting to admit this is what I think it is

—the close of the game, the brick wall at the end of the alley, too high to climb.

I wake up later—not sure how much later, but the light in the room is brighter—and the world is steady again, but my arm is even more numb than it was before. I clench my fist and release it, again and again. I watch my hand move sluggishly back and forth, but I can't grip my blanket between my fingers, and soon the headache that felt like it was going to crack my skull open on the way back from Caitlin's house last night, returns.

I lie in bed for a long time, head throbbing like a thumb with a splinter shoved beneath the nail, knowing I should get up and ask my mother or father to help me take a pain pill. But I dread the scene I'll cause when I confess I can't open the bottle myself. It will all be over, then. There will be no more hiding from it, even if the numbness goes away.

Please go away. Please. I need a little more time.

No, I need a lot more time. I need a lifetime. I need a future to promise her, but what you need, and what you get, are rarely the same thing. This is what I have—a numb arm, a pounding head, and unfinished business I need to get out of bed and take care of before it's too late.

I shove my sheet and blanket to the end of the bed and lie beneath the swirling ceiling fan in nothing but my boxer briefs, hoping the cool air will help banish the pounding sensation in my head.

It works…a little, and in a few minutes I feel good enough to sit up and reach for my phone.

I text Caitlin, punching in my message with my left thumb, trying not to think about what happens if my left arm starts playing the same kind of games as my right. Less than a minute later, she texts me back, saying she can't get away this afternoon, but I'm welcome to come over to her house early.

Be there as soon as I can, I text back. *I want us to find someplace private to talk. Not in front of the kids.*

Okay. The dots flicker on my phone, indicating she's typing something lengthy, but when the rest of the message comes through it's simply: *Everything okay?*

No, it's not okay. I've promised things I had no business promising. And now I'll have to pay the price, and so will Caitlin. But I can't tell her that in a text, so I simply punch in—

I'll explain when I get there.

—and turn off my phone.

I force myself out of bed and shuffle into the bathroom where I take a shower, feeling only half in my body as I make accommodations for my numb arm without thinking too much about what I'm doing. I shave and dress, refusing to look my reflection in the eye. If I look myself in the eye there will be no more hiding. I will slip out of this fuzzy state of shock, and slip into a very different emotional state. One that won't be conducive to ending things with the only girl I've ever loved, and that won't be any good for anyone.

It's time to end it—quickly, cleanly—to cut myself off from Caitlin like a rotten limb before I can further infect her life.

I tell my parents I'm going for a drive and will be back before dinner, leaving the sitting room without answering my mother's inquiry as to how I'm feeling. That's another conversation better left until after I've finished my business at the Cooney house; I doubt my parents would be keen on me driving without feeling in one arm.

I have to stop twice on the way across town. Once, because the highway starts shifting on its axis, and I have to pull over until the world steadies; once a few blocks from Caitlin's house, to firm up what I'm going to say. I thought I'd have more time, but now we're suddenly at the finish line and I haven't had a chance to prepare.

All I know is that I have to make her hate me. If we'd made it to the end of the summer, we might have been able to part as friends, but now alienating her is the only option. I don't want her coming after me, searching for an explanation as to why I've suddenly gone back on our bargain. She knows me too well, and knows keeping my promises is impor-tant to me. She would put her clever, stubborn head to work figuring out what I'm hiding and it wouldn't be difficult for her to find out.

Hating me is the only thing that will keep her out of my business, and away from Darby Hill, where my mother is waiting to spill all of my secrets. My father can be trusted to keep his mouth shut—he likes Caitlin, and will see that what I've done is for the best—so there shouldn't be any problem with him continuing to represent her in her suit against her father.

She'll get custody of the kids, have enough money to go back to school, and be able to truly move on with her life. She'll be able to keep the good things from our time together, without suffering the fallout. She might be upset for a while —sometimes, I think she cares for me more than she lets on—but she'll get over a broken heart. She's only twenty years old. She has her entire life ahead of her, a life she'll spend loving someone much better for her than me.

The thought sends a wave a pain flashing through my body that has nothing to do with the nightmare in my head.

I park in front of her house and shut off the engine, taking a moment to brace myself.

Before I can get out of the car, the front door slams open and Sean flies out, followed closely by Emmie, wearing the rainbow tutu Caitlin and I bought her at the French Heritage festival last weekend. She is smiling that smile that looks so much like Caitlin's, looking so sweet and innocent and obviously happy to see me that it flays at my insides.

My heart squeezes and my chest is suddenly so tight I can barely draw a breath. It's not just Caitlin I love. I love that little girl. I love the way she looks at me like I'm something completely good, a hero.

But I'm no hero. I'm a monster. I'm as bad as the people in Dad's files, lying to myself and everyone around me. Trying to make it okay to take what I want without stopping to think of the people I'm destroying along the way.

The kids won't be destroyed. They're young. Emmie will forget you in a week, the boys in two or three. It's not too late for a clean break.

My ribs loosen. I draw a deep breath, force a smile, and exit the car. I ruffle Sean's hair as I pass him by, and stop long enough to lean down, pressing a soft kiss to Emmie's forehead, but I don't stop to ask about their day, or where they want to go for a drive after dinner the way I usually do.

"We'll be in the backyard," Sean calls out after me, a plaintive note in his voice that makes me think he realizes something's wrong. "Come out after you talk to Caitlin."

"We'll see," I say noncommittally, determined not to lie to the Cooney kids any more than I have already. I trudge up the concrete steps to the house, letting myself in without bothering to knock. I'm allowed to do that now; I'm practically part of the family.

The thought makes me wince as I shut the door behind me.

"Be down in just a second!" Caitlin calls from upstairs.

Her voice is a knife slipped between my ribs. I would rather die than do what I came here to do. I don't want to hurt her. I want to give her the world, fight for her dreams, promise her forever. I want to spend my life making her happy, making her laugh, making her come—crying out my name in that voice that is my favorite voice because it is hers.

God, I love her, so fucking much, but I'm not much better than a ghost.

But she's still alive—even more alive than the day I met her—and her potential is limitless. I believe in her, more than I've ever believed in anyone, and that's why I will do this. Because to do anything else would hurt more than the verbal blows I'll deliver today.

She pounds down the stairs a split second after my resolve has slipped into place, Danny not far behind her.

"Sorry, we were fixing the toilet. It broke again and…" Her words trail away as our eyes meet across the living room. Her smile fades and fear flickers in her eyes. "What's wrong?"

"We need to talk," I say, voice flat, emotionless.

"Danny go outside," Caitlin says softly, throat working as she swallows.

"But I was going to play—"

"Go outside," Caitlin repeats more firmly. "Please. And keep everyone else outside until I say it's okay to come back in."

Danny hesitates, glancing between me and Caitlin. After a moment, something shifts in his expression and he nods. "Oh…okay."

He turns to leave, but before he reaches the kitchen he turns back. "Are you sure you don't want me to stay,

LILI VALENTE

Caitlin? Watch your back?" he asks, shooting me a narrow look, a look that is full of anger and disbelief and a silent prayer not to do what he knows I'm going to do. What we all know I'm going to do.

Caitlin shakes her head. "No…but thanks, D."

"All right," Danny says. "Call me if you need me."

"Will do," Caitlin says to him, but she's looking at me, watching me like a loaded gun.

I hold her gaze, wanting to make it clear from the beginning that there are no cracks in my resolve. There will be no backing down, no bargaining, no buying time. This is the end. The train stops here and everyone but me is getting off before it jumps the tracks.

I wait until I hear the back door close behind Danny to say, "I talked to my father this morning about what will happen when you get custody of the kids. It's forever. You understand that, right?"

She nods, but doesn't say a word.

"You'll be legally bound to take care of them until Emmie's eighteen," I say. "You'll be signing half your life away."

"I know," she says.

I sigh. "Listen, I like you, Caitlin, a lot, and lately I've been thinking this thing between us could be serious, but I'm not ready to take on a family. I don't want to sacrifice the best years of my life because your parents and sister can't be bothered to live up to their responsibilities. I have bigger dreams."

Caitlin's brows draw together, hurt and shock

mixing in her eyes. "Yeah, I know that, Gabe. From the beginning, we both agreed this was just for the summer."

"It's becoming more than that, and you know it." I say, forcing irritation into my tone. "The kids are getting attached; you're getting attached."

"Don't tell me what I'm feeling," she snaps.

"It's better if we end it now before we get in any deeper." I take a step toward the door, even though all I want to do is cross the room, pull her into my arms, and kiss her until we both forget everything I've said. "Despite what some people think, I'm not a heartless asshole. I don't want to be responsible for making kids cry when I skip town in August and never come back."

"So that's it?" she asks, voice breaking. "It's over. Just like that?"

"I think a clean break is best." I shrug. "My father is still going to represent you for free, and the money in the joint account in Charleston is yours. I'll send you something later this week letting you know where the rest of the cash is hidden. Altogether, it should be enough to cover expenses while you get your degree."

Caitlin nods and keeps nodding for a long time. She crosses her arms, uncrosses them, drops her gaze to the carpet, and then tilts her head back to stare at the ceiling. She laughs softly, and runs a hand through her hair, but still doesn't say a word.

"I really do wish you all the best," I say, speaking

the truth for the first time since I walked in the door.

Caitlin pulls in a breath that emerges as a sob. "I don't believe you."

"It's the truth. I think you're a good person, who deserves good things."

"No, not that," she says, voice vibrating with anger as she crosses the room, getting close enough for me to smell her Caitlin smell, breaking my heart a little more as I realize this is the last time I'll ever breathe her in.

"I don't believe the kids are why you're calling it off," she continues, pinning me with a wounded look. "I see the way you smile at them. You care about them, and you're *happy* when you're with our family. That's not fake, I know it's not."

"Caring, and wanting to play daddy, are two very different things."

"Bullshit," she says, eyes shining with unshed tears. "You're happy here; you're happy with me, and you said you weren't going back to college, anyway. What other plans can you have that are worth setting everything we have on fire and walking away?"

"I'm sorry if I led you to believe I was feeling something that I don't," I say, my voice stiff.

She laughs, sending the tears in her eyes gliding down her cheeks. "You *do* feel something. You love me; I know you do. And I love you." Her face crumples for a moment before she sucks in a breath, regaining control. "I love you so much it scares me to death, but I'm not running away. I'm not being a coward."

"You can't run." I cross my arms, fighting the urge to reach for her, to crush her to my chest and tell her love isn't a strong enough word for what I feel for her. "You're tied to the kids, to this town. You couldn't run away, even if you wanted to."

"I could," she says in a softer voice. "I could drop the suit, give Chuck the kids, and come with you, wherever you're going."

"You wouldn't," I say, searching her face, afraid she might be serious.

She lifts her chin, and swipes the tears from her cheek with a rough palm. "My mom and sister did it, and somebody always stepped in to pick up the pieces. I could do it, too."

"You know there's no one left to step in," I whisper, casting a glance toward the backyard, where the kids are playing. "You're the only person any of them can count on. If you left, you'd destroy them."

"So?" Caitlin says. "Maybe I'm tired of being the girl people can count on."

I shake my head, a scowl clawing into my face as my skull starts to pound all over again. "You'd break their hearts. Maybe forever. Can you really fucking live with that?"

Caitlin smiles, a slow, trembling smile that tells me I've walked into a trap. "You should see the look on your face. You *really* look like a guy who doesn't give a shit about those kids."

I squeeze my eyes shut and drive a hand through my hair, cussing beneath my breath.

"You love them," Caitlin says, hope thick in her voice. "And I love them, and I love you, and I know we can be good together. We could…we could even be family." Her hands come to my chest, her fingers fisting in my gray tee shirt. It's the same one I was wearing when I asked her to come play with me, back when I was still dumb enough to believe this thing with Caitlin could remain a casual, summer fling. "Stay with me, Gabe. Don't run. Stay. Please."

I open my eyes. Her face is so close, and I want to kiss her so badly I can taste the sweetness I know I'll find in her mouth, but I can't. I can't kiss her, I can't keep loving her, I can't stay here or I'm going to ruin everything.

If I stay, I'll carry her upstairs and make love to her. I'll hold her close after, and confess it all, and she'll still want me to stay because she is kind and generous and strong, but it will destroy her. *I* will destroy her, and I can't have that on my conscience. I have no illusions about going to heaven—I don't even know if I believe in it anymore—but I want to go out clean, without emotional blood on my hands. I won't give Caitlin and the kids a front row seat to more pointless suffering. They've been through enough. I have to finish this, or I will never forgive myself.

"Sometimes love isn't enough," I say roughly. I cover her fists with my fingers and force her hands away. "I like you, and I love fucking you, but you are not what I want, Caitlin. I don't want this."

"You're a liar," she says, but there is doubt in her voice and fresh tears stream down her cheeks.

"I *am* a liar, and a thief, and a sociopath," I say. "And I don't plan to change. Is that really who you want helping you raise the kids?"

"Yes, because you're also a good man," she says, with a ferocity that surprises me. "And because I'm all of those things, too."

"Only because I've messed you up," I say. "You'll be better off when I'm gone."

"No, I won't." She shakes her head hard enough to send her hair flying around her shoulders. "I don't want to go back to who I was before. I don't care if the old Caitlin was a better version of me; I want to be the person I am with you. I want to feel this alive and happy and whole. I won't go back, even if you walk out that door right now."

"But please...please stay." Her forehead wrinkles and her tear-filled eyes squeeze shut and I can feel her pain like it's my own, because it is.

She isn't the only one who feels like a piece of her body is being ripped away. She's a part of me now, the best part, and for the first time in my life I don't feel alone. And she feels the same, I can see it in her eyes, feel it vibrating in the air around us. I've met my perfect match, and we're in love.

The irony that it happened now is enough to crush my heart to bloody pieces.

"I can't." I choke out as I turn toward the door.

"You *won't*," she counters with a sob.

"Same difference," I say, hand closing around the door handle. "I'm leaving town soon. I don't want to see you again. Don't come by my house, don't call, don't contact me, or my family, unless you have a question for my father about your case."

She draws in a shuddering breath, but before she can say another word, I push through the door into the summer heat. It's only then—as I'm rushing across the patchy lawn with the sun beating down hard enough to make beads of sweat pop on my upper lip—that I realize the air conditioning had been on inside the house.

I've been telling her to turn it on for weeks, promising it was safe to let down her guard, to stop hoarding every cent, and spend some money on things that will make her and the kids more comfortable.

It seems she finally took my advice, just in time for me to prove she should never have listened to a bastard like me.

CHAPTER 23

CAITLIN

If it's drowning you're after,
don't torment yourself with shallow water. –Irish
Proverb

I don't know how long I sit on the couch and cry after he leaves. It seems like hours, and only a few moments, all at the same time. The pain is so intense it feels like it's been eating away at me forever, and so sharp it's as if the knife is just sliding in—fresh and agonizing.

I cry and cry, but it doesn't make the hurt go away. It doesn't even take the edge off. I know I'm wasting time and energy, but I can't stop. I am broken, and thanks to Gabe I don't know how to put myself back together again. The old Caitlin would have already swallowed all these feelings and started throwing something together for dinner—

since hamburger night has clearly fallen through. Old Caitlin would have put inconvenient emotions aside for later, put her chin up, and soldiered on.

No, old Caitlin would never have had these emotions in the first place. She didn't let down her guard; she didn't invite strangers in. She didn't know what it was like to hold Gabe's hand, to laugh with him over a dozen private jokes, to look into his eyes while he moved above her and see the pleasure-pain in his expression as they made love.

Pleasure, because every time Gabe and I touch it is magic; pain because it's almost too beautiful, too perfect, too close. When Gabe and I make love, I know he can see into every corner of my heart, every dark hollow in my soul. He takes me all in, every twisted piece, and reflects an image so beautiful, I had started to believe his reflection was the true one. I had started to believe I was lovable, and that Gabe was going to change his mind and stay with me, no matter what kind of plans he'd made, no matter how stubborn he is once he has set his mind on something.

Deep down, I'd thought I was enough to hold him, and be everything he'd ever need.

I still can't believe I was so wrong. I saw the way Gabe looked at me; I felt the reverence in his touch. He never touched me like something he planned to throw away. He touched me like what we had was sacred. I know he's an amazing liar, but I didn't think even he was *this* good, so good I'd have no clue he was checking out until the rug was yanked out from beneath me and I was already flying through the air.

Guess that's what happens when you fall in love with a sociopath, I think, but that word doesn't sit any better in my head than it did in my heart when Gabe used it as an excuse to walk away.

Gabe might be a sociopath; *I* might be a sociopath—I probably am, it would go a long way to explaining why I don't feel bad about any of the things Gabe and I have done—but that doesn't mean we don't have a code. There are certain things I would never do. I would never abandon my family, I would never hurt an innocent, and I would never kick someone while they were down.

Aside from the conversation we had when I drew the line at robbery, forbidding other criminal activity, Gabe and I never sat down to talk about morals or ethics, but I felt in my gut that we saw things the same way. Gabe is blunt, but he's never cruel. He's self-interested, but never selfish—quite the opposite in fact. I know he would have given me every dime in his trust fund if I'd asked for it. He's changeable, but his promises mean something. He doesn't give his word or strike a deal unless he intends to follow through.

"So why is he backing out now?" I whisper, my voice thick from crying.

I stand, suddenly full of restless energy, and move into the kitchen. I grab a tissue and blow my nose, mop up my face, and think about the question.

Why *is* he backing out now? Something must have changed...but what?

It's not the kids; that smelled like a lie from beginning to end. It's not because we're falling in love. We've been falling in love for weeks. If he was going to run because he was getting too close, my gut says he would have run the night he found out he was my first. But he didn't run; he stayed and made love to me again, and slept over, and continued to sleep over almost every night since.

We've had innocent fun on the weekends with the kids, and wicked fun late at night, just the two of us—planning jobs, pulling them off, and coming home to celebrate naked in my bed. The only thing we've ever fought about is whether or not to waste money turning on the air conditioning, and that's no reason to break up, especially not considering I finally turned the fucking thing on last night.

I pace back and forth in the kitchen, running through every moment of the six weeks we spent together, but out of all the memories we've made, the only moment that sets my radar to blipping is last night.

Last night, when Gabe was acting so strangely. Last night, when he was dizzy, and would have been caught if I hadn't been there to help him.

Could that be it? Is he afraid we're going to get caught? If that's it, a part of me insists this rift will be easy to fix. We can simply stop pulling jobs and be a normal couple—problem solved.

But I know it's not that easy. The jobs are as

much a part of me and Gabe as the jokes and the family burger nights and the way we make love like we were made to give each other pleasure. The rush I feel when I'm in my blacks and Gabe and I are whispering through our last minute checklist is as sweet as the kisses after. I love everything that makes us *us*, and that includes giving the horrible people we've robbed a little of what they deserve. Giving up pulling jobs together would be like giving up making love. Our relationship would suffer, wither, and eventually become something less than it was before.

Maybe Gabe has already figured that out. Maybe he's realized that the rush is an integral part of who we are as a couple, but that there's no way to keep doing what we do without eventually getting caught. Maybe he's finally realized what I've known since the beginning—that he might not always be able to protect me, no matter how honest his intentions.

And maybe *that's* why he's doing this. He's calling things off before I get caught or hurt, and the kids suffer the consequences. *That* would make sense with the Gabe I know, the one who's come to care about my brothers and Emmie, and who realizes I'm the only thing standing between them and a hard life none of them deserve.

"But it's my choice," I say, dampening the edge of a dishtowel, and using it to wipe my sticky, tear-streaked face.

It *is* my choice, and my life, and I should be the

275

one who gets to decide whether the risk is worth the reward. And Gabe should know better than to think I'm going to let him make my decisions for me. The only time he calls the shots is in the bedroom, and that's not even completely accurate. He takes the lead when we're naked because I *allow* him to take the lead. I'm still in control, and we're still a team, even when I'm following his directions and making myself vulnerable to him.

And if I'm right and Gabe is really sacrificing everything we have because he's decided this isn't good for me, then this conversation isn't over. I'll fight for him the same way I fight for the kids, because he is precious and irreplaceable and I can't bear the thought of never seeing his face again.

The frightened, helpless feeling that turned my stomach to acid when Gabe walked out the door subsides, replaced by resolve to keep fighting until I get through to the pig-headed man I love. With a final sniff, I grab a pitcher of lemonade from the fridge and cups from the cupboard and head out into the backyard.

Outside, the sun is lower in the sky than I expect it to be and the kids are unusually subdued. Sean is still half-heartedly kicking the soccer ball around the perimeter of the fence, but Danny and Ray are lying on a blanket in the shade reading comic books, with Emmie asleep next to them, her flushed cheek resting on Danny's leg and her thumb popped between her lips.

I set the lemonade on the picnic table and perch

on the edge of the seat, grateful for the shade and the breeze that drifts through the backyard, cooling my flushed skin in a way even the air conditioning in the house couldn't seem to manage.

"Hey," I say softly to Ray and Danny, not wanting to wake Emmie. "How do you guys feel about chicken tonight? We could go into town and hit Charlie's, get a bucket of chicken and some rolls, and eat it in the park."

Ray looks up from his comic book, brows furrowed. "What about burger night?"

"Burger night's cancelled," Danny says bitterly, not lifting his eyes from the page he's on. "Gabe bailed."

"Gabe didn't bail," I lie. "He's just...sorting through some things. I'm going to go talk to him tomorrow before I go into work."

"So we can have burger night some other night?" Ray asks.

"Sure. You guys want some lemonade? It's nice and cool."

Danny grunts. "Screw lemonade. And screw burger night."

"Language, Danny," I say, but I'm too tired to muster up a threatening tone.

"Gabe isn't coming back," Danny says, snapping his comic book closed. "I saw the look on his face. He's done with us."

"If he's done with anyone, it's me," I say. "This has nothing to do with you. Gabe cares about all of you. So much."

"If he cares so much, why did he dump you?" Danny asks.

I frown. "Who says he dumped me?"

Danny looks up at the leaves swaying overhead, lips tight around the edges. "The phone rang about an hour ago. It keep ringing and ringing, so I went in to answer it. I thought you'd gone out front or something, but you were on the couch crying."

"Oh," I say, sighing. "I'm sorry."

"You were so out of it you didn't even hear the phone," Danny says flatly, in that voice that I know means something has scared him and he's trying hard not to show it. "I asked you if you were okay, but you didn't hear me, either. So I just grabbed the comic books and came back outside."

"I'm sorry," I say again. "I was upset." I take a deep breath. "But I'm better now, and I think Gabe and I can sort this out."

Danny finally looks away from the leaves. "It's just weird," he says, the hurt in his eyes making my stomach ache. "I mean...everything seemed fine."

"I know," I agree, mouth pulling to one side as I fight a wave of emotion. "I know it did."

"I hate surprises," Ray says in a soft voice. "That's why I like books. Even if things are bad for a long time, the good guys always win in the end."

"Not in all books," I say. "Literary fiction usually ends pretty badly."

Ray shrugs. "That's why I'm not going to read those. I like books I can trust."

I smile. "I like those, too."

Danny sighs. "I'd rather play video games. Is it cool if I go in?"

"Yeah. Let me help you with Emmie." I slip off the bench onto the blanket, gently holding Emmie while Danny shifts his leg free, before easing her back onto the blanket. She whimpers in her sleep, but doesn't wake up, so I settle down beside her, knowing nothing will help ease the ache in my chest like watching Emmie sleep.

"Don't get in too deep with anything," I warn Danny as he stands. "I'm going to bring everyone in to get cleaned up to go out to dinner in thirty minutes. I'll call the house phone from my cell and let it ring once so you'll know to turn off the blood and guts."

Danny nods, and starts to go before stopping and turning back. "That reminds me, the phone call earlier was weird."

"How so?" I swipe a stray curl from Emmie's forehead.

"It was some guy. He asked if you were home, and I said yeah, did he want to talk to you, but then he just hung up."

I look back at him, brows drawing together. "He didn't give his name?"

Danny shakes his head. "No, he just hung up."

I hum, wondering who in the world would be calling for me. Gabe and Isaac are the only boys who ever call and Isaac is mad at me, and Gabe told me he was never going to contact me again.

"But it sounded like somebody I know," Danny adds. "The voice was familiar."

"One of Dad's friends, maybe?" I ask. "The ones that used to come over before he moved in with Veronica?"

Danny shrugs. "I don't know. But it was weird. I'm not answering the phone anymore. I'm going to let it fucking ring until someone else gets it."

"Language," I say automatically, but as Danny rolls his eyes and heads inside, my mind is still on the phone call.

I guess it could be someone from work, but Harry and Carlos are the only men at the diner and neither of them would call and not leave their names. Some of the guys at the movie theater, however, are perpetually stoned, even when they're running the popcorn machine. They might have called to see if I could cover a shift, forgetting that I quit my job at the theater until after they had Danny on the phone.

But what if it's someone else...maybe even a mark who has figured out I was on their property? It's a long shot—Gabe and I were always so careful —but even a chance one of the monsters we've targeted called my house is enough.

I decide to invest in a security system tomorrow morning, and put the phone call momentarily out of mind.

I take the kids out to eat and play at the park, then herd everyone home and get them bathed and in P.J.s and in bed by ten. Then, I spend two hours on our ancient computer researching sociopaths, and decide the term doesn't apply to either Gabe or me. Gabe never tried to manipulate me or turn me into a victim. Gabe never took pleasure in hurting me. Even today, when he was trying to be so hard, I could tell it was killing him to say the things he did.

I decide that, whatever Gabe and I are, it's something gentler than a sociopath. Or that sociopathic tendencies must cover a wide spectrum. Maybe being a sociopath is less like a skyscraper hotel with cookie-cutter rooms, and more like a lake surrounded by individual cabins, each one with its own unique characteristics, but very similar views.

I'm not sure what to think, but I feel more informed, and less alone. The fact that I'm comforted that there are thousands of people in the world like me and Gabe—high functioning, intelligent people who enjoy breaking society's rules, and rarely feel guilty about it—is probably confirmation that I'm somewhere on the sociopath spectrum, but by the time I snap the laptop closed, I'm too sleepy to care.

I trudge upstairs to the bathroom, wash my face, and brush my teeth. I change into the sleep shirt I hung on the back of the door this morning—the pink one Gabe hates—and head toward bed, exhaustion tugging at the backs of my eyes. I'm still torn up about what happened today, but I'm also hopeful that I'll be able to get through to Gabe tomorrow. As far as I'm concerned, morning can't come soon enough.

I open my door, so focused on getting my head on the pillow that I don't see the shadow standing in the corner of the darkened room until he's almost on top of me.

I freeze, lifting my hands to defend myself even as I open my mouth to scream, but then there is an explosion of pain and a flash of light behind my left eye. The world goes fuzzy around the edges, my knees turn to jelly, and I slide to the ground with a whimper, holding on to consciousness just long enough to hear Ned Pitt's nasal voice whisper—

"You've been a bad girl, Miss Cooney."

And then I black out, terror following me into the dark.

Gabe and Caitlin's story continues in
A Love So Deadly. Available Now

And subscribe to Lili's newsletter HERE **to make sure you never miss a sale or new release.**

SNEAK PEEK

Please enjoy this sneak peek of
A LOVE SO DEADLY
To the Bone Book Two
Available Now

Gabe

The course of true love never did run smooth. -
Shakespeare

I can't sleep.

I lie in bed for hours, but I can't sleep and I can't
quit thinking about her.

It's all I've done all day. I keep seeing her face in
that moment before I bolted, with her cheeks
flushed and wet with tears, and the shattered look
in her eyes. I keep hearing the way her voice

cracked when she told me she loved me, feeling the hairline fractures in my heart getting wider and wider.

She loves me; I love her.

She needs me; I need her.

All the other truths keep swirling around in my head, insisting they're relevant, but in the end it comes back to loving and needing and wondering why doing the right thing feels so wrong. I tell myself that this hurt now will spare her bigger hurt later, but as I lie in the darkness, watching my ceiling fan spin in circles, a voice deep inside insists I haven't given Caitlin the credit she deserves.

Life has knocked her down again and again, but she keeps getting back up. Her dad is a waste, but Caitlin never let that be an excuse to give up on making her life better. Her mom abandoned the family when Caitlin was twelve, and Caitlin stepped up and helped her older sister take care of the younger kids. Her sister left when Caitlin was seventeen, and Caitlin stood strong and stubbornly refused to let her family fall apart.

A month ago, I would have said she sacrificed herself for the kids, but now I know that's not accurate. Caitlin is a good person, but she doesn't do anything she doesn't want to do. She did what she did because, at the end of the day, the people she loves mean more to her than anything else in the world. Those kids are her biggest source of pride, their happiness the soul food that keeps her going.

Her love isn't a stone tied around her neck; it's the source of her impressive strength.

She is tougher than anyone in her life gives her credit for—even me.

Chances are she's tough enough to hear my truth, and to walk the last steps along the road with me. In my heart, I know she'd want to do it. She'd want to know that I wasn't alone, that the most important person in my life was with me. And she has to know that person is her, that she is…everything.

I was certain she did, but that was before I took a chainsaw to her heart earlier today.

I squeeze my eyes closed and curse beneath my breath.

Have I fucked things up again? Have I made everything worse, when all I was trying to do was make the kindest choice possible?

I wish I had parents like the ones on the television shows I loved as a kid. I wish I had someone I could trust to give me good advice. But Aaron and Deborah have never been my kind of people. We might as well be from two different planets, as was evidenced when I got back from Caitlin's house late this afternoon and confessed to my parents that my symptoms were getting worse.

My mom spent approximately two minutes sniffling before heading into her office to arrange for plane flights and reservations for the hospice I picked out when I decided not to go through with the surgery. I sat in silence with my dad, listening to my mother's voice drift into the sitting room until I heard her place a call to her interior decorator, to discuss having my room packed up and remodeled.

Not quite ready to contemplate every trace of my existence being wiped away, I left. My father, who I know will never forgive me for "giving up," didn't even say goodbye.

I know they love me. I know they aren't as cold as they appear—this is just how they deal with their feelings of powerlessness and grief—but I don't want my mother's or father's eyes to be the last thing I see. I want to be looking into Caitlin's green eyes, the only eyes that have ever seen every secret part of me, the eyes of the only person who has ever made me feel normal, whole, and completely loved.

I turn things over and over and still can't decide what the right answer is, but I know I can't stay in bed a second longer. I shove off the sheets and swing my legs down to the floor, ignoring the faint aching in my skull. The pain has remained under control since I took a pill after getting back from Caitlin's, and I haven't had another dizzy spell since right after dinner. I should be okay to drive, and even if I weren't, I'd still go. I suddenly need to get out of the house. I have to *go* somewhere, even if I'm not sure where I'm headed.

Or so I tell myself.

I tell myself I'm just going for a drive, but I'm not surprised when I find myself steering the Beamer toward Caitlin's. It's after midnight and I doubt she's awake—and I'm not ready to go back on my decision to end it—but looking at the darkened house and knowing she's inside will be more comforting than any other view in Giffney.

I turn off the headlights before I pull onto her street, not wanting her to see them sweep across the curtains if she's still awake. I let the car idle almost noiselessly halfway around the cul-de-sac before I roll down my window, shove the car into park, and cut the engine.

Seconds later, the car parked in front of me— a dark sedan with a dent on one side of the roof —roars to life. The driver swerves away from the curb, tires squealing as he pulls away and guns it toward the stop sign at the end of the road. I flick on my lights, figuring the psycho must be smashed, and I should get his plate in case he hits someone, when I see a piece of threadbare fabric peeking out of the sedan's trunk.

The fabric is bright pink, a garish color that's horribly familiar.

It's the same color as the fat cat tee shirt Caitlin loves to wear to bed. The shirt is three sizes too big, and so thin from washing that it's transparent. Normally I would approve, but the obese cat sprawled across the front of the shirt, scratching his balls, negates any sex appeal.

I see the flash of fabric, and immediately, in my mind, Caitlin is in that trunk. Caitlin is being kidnapped by a man in a dark blue sedan driving like a maniac.

A man I might lose if I don't follow him. Right. Fucking. Now.

I twist the key and slam the Beamer into drive, shooting off after the sedan, catching sight of him as he pulls right onto Newberry, headed away from downtown. I stop at the stop sign, cursing the white minivan that shoots past, coming between me and the sedan. As soon as the van is clear, I turn, fingers squeezing the steering wheel as my heart pounds and my mouth goes dry with fear. I weave over the center line, keeping the car, and that scrap of pink fabric, in my sight.

A voice in my head says I'm being crazy, but I can't shake the feeling that Caitlin's in trouble. I can't see much more than an outline of the driver's head, but it's obviously a man driving the car. And why the fuck would a man have pink fabric, the exact horrible shade as Caitlin's tee shirt, in his trunk?

He's got a daughter who plays soccer, and she left her jersey in the trunk. He's got a wife who boxed up a load of clothes to take to the Salvation Army and he hasn't gotten around to dropping them off yet.

There are lots of reasons. But none of them explain why this strange car was parked outside of Caitlin's house in the middle of the night, and is driving like a bat out of hell.

I back off the minivan's ass, easing off the pedal until I'm a respectable two car lengths away, and slip in my Bluetooth earpiece. I voice dial Caitlin's landline, but keep my eyes on the sedan. The driver has slowed and is keeping the car between the lines, but he's still going at least ten miles over the limit.

Why is he in such a hurry? There is hardly anyone on the road this time of night, and Giffney isn't that big. He's going to get where he's going soon enough sticking to forty miles per hour.

The phone rings and rings, until finally I'm sent to the answering machine.

"This is Gabe," I say. "Caitlin, I need you to call me back. Right away."

I end the call and redial immediately. The phone rings, and the answering machine picks up, but just as I'm leaving another message for Caitlin, Danny picks up the phone.

"What the fuck," he says, his voice slurred with sleep. "It's the middle of the fucking night, asshole. Haven't you made my sister cry enough for one day?"

Something inside me cringes thinking about Caitlin crying, but there's no time to apologize. "Danny, listen to me. I need you to go upstairs and get your sister."

"Fuck you," he says.

"Danny, please," I insist, panic that he might hang up straining my voice. "Please, just…go make sure she's up there. You don't have to wake her. Just make sure she's safe, and come back and let me know."

Danny mumbles something I can't understand, but I'm assuming is more profanity.

"Please, Danny," I beg, fist tightening around the

wheel as I make a sharp left turn onto county road 50, following the sedan as he takes the back roads out of town. "I'm worried about her. I'll drop a hundred dollar bill in the mailbox for you tomorrow, if you'll just let me know she's upstairs sleeping."

"Keep your money," he snaps.

There's a sharp clacking sound, loud enough to make me wince, but the line doesn't go dead. I strain to hear what's going on and imagine I can make out Danny's footsteps thudding up the stairs. A minute passes—a minute that I know is a minute, not an eternity, because I can see the clock on my console holding steady at 12:21—and then I definitely hear footsteps on the stairs.

The steps are faster, louder, giving me a clue that Caitlin isn't safe in her bed, even before a breathless Danny picks up the phone.

"She's not there," he pants, not sounding so tough anymore. He sounds as scared as I feel, and so young I feel like shit for not being able to protect him from whatever has happened. "She's not in bed and the lamp near the window is knocked over. The bulb is shattered all over the floor."

I curse, fingers tightening on the wheel, barely resisting the urge to slam the gas pedal closer to the floor and shorten the distance between me and the sedan. But if this guy has Caitlin, he's going to be on the lookout for someone following him. I don't want to get into a high speed chase with the girl I love knocking around in the trunk. She could already be hurt. I need to keep my thoughts clear, and my head on straight, and do whatever it takes to make sure I get her back in one piece.

And make sure I have the chance to tear the man who took her into strips of bleeding, aching, dying flesh for daring to touch her. I'll kill him if he's hurt her.

I may kill him anyway.

"I'm going to call 911," Danny says, pulling my thoughts back to the boy on the other end of the line.

"No, wait," I say, though a part of me insists it's a good idea.

But I don't know who has Caitlin, or what he might know about our extracurricular activities. There's a chance that her kidnapping is unrelated to the things we've been doing, but I can't know that for sure, and until I do, I can't put her future at risk. I don't want the cops called in until I'm sure I can't handle this myself.

"Wait until I get a better idea of where this guy is going," I say. "I'm following the man who took her."

"What?" Danny says. "How?"

"I pulled up outside your house as the man was pulling away. I saw part of Caitlin's pink tee shirt sticking out of the trunk."

Danny curses. "What are you going to do? You have to get her back, Gabe."

"I'm going to get her back," I promise. "Hang tight by the phone. If I need you to call the police, I'll call. If you don't hear from me in twenty minutes, get one of the cell phones from Caitlin's bedside table. Call 911 from the cell, and leave an anonymous tip that you saw a blue sedan headed east on route 50. Tell them you heard a girl screaming inside the trunk. Don't tell them who you are."

"Can you hear her screaming?" Danny asks, his voice shaking.

"No, I can't," I say softly. "I'm going to drive now, Danny. Hang in there, don't tell any of the other kids, and don't give your name to the police. I'm going to bring Caitlin home, or die trying."

"Okay," Danny says. A moment later the line goes dead, seconds before the sedan takes a sharp turn to the left, headed down a gravel road.

I fight the urge to brake, keeping the Beamer headed straight on 50 even though my heart surges up into my throat as I watch the car with Caitlin in it rush away to the north. That last turn was too sudden, even for a crap driver like this guy. He must suspect I'm following him. I have to keep going until the next bend, then turn around and retrace my route with the headlights off and put him off his guard. I should be able to figure out where he went. It hasn't rained in weeks. The gravel is dry and will hang in the air after being disturbed. All I'll have to do is hang back and follow the trail.

Around the next turn, I veer onto the shoulder and spin in a tight circle, flipping my lights off as I start back the way I came. It's dark as the bottom level of hell out here in the country, away from the lights of town and the streetlights of the suburbs. But there's a half moon in the sky, giving off enough light that I'm able to keep the car on the right side of the road. I spot the turn onto the gravel road—Ellery Avenue—and turn right.

My heart is still beating so fast and hard it feels like someone is punching me in the throat with every throb of my pulse, but the knowledge that I'm back on the fucker's trail is comforting. So is the haze of dust hanging in the air above the road. I'm starting to think this is going to work, and I'll be able to tail the guy to wherever he's taking Caitlin without being observed, when a lightning bolt of pain zigzags through my skull.

It starts in my neck and rips through the center of my head to explode behind my right eye. I see dying stars—flashes of orange and deep red that morph into patches of blinding white light—and the world does a three sixty.

I cry out and slam on the brakes.

Or, I think I do. I tell my foot to push down, but I'm not sure if it obeys. I'm not sure where I am, who I am. All I know is that I'm blind and the world is spinning. Up is down, right is left, I can't see and I can't nail down my position in space. And then, like a light switched off, everything goes black, and I am alone with the pain that roars inside me like a monster hungry for blood.

A Love so Deadly is
Available Now

TELL LILI YOUR FAVORITE PART!

I love reading your thoughts about the books and your review matters. Reviews help readers find new-to-them authors to enjoy. So if you could take a moment to leave a review letting me know your favorite part of the story—nothing fancy required, even a sentence or two would be wonderful—I would be deeply grateful.

ABOUT THE AUTHOR

Author of over forty novels, *USA Today* Bestseller **Lili Valente** writes everything from steamy suspense to laugh-out-loud romantic comedies. A die-hard romantic, she can't resist a story where love wins big. Because love should always win. She lives in Vermont with her two big-hearted boy children and a dog named Pippa Jane.

Find Lili at...
www.lilivalente.com

ALSO BY LILI VALENTE

The McGuire Brothers

Boss Without Benefits

Not Today Bossman

Boss Me Around

When It Pours (novella)

Kind of a Sexy Jerk

When it Shines (novella)

Kind of a Hot Mess

Kind of a Dirty Talker

Kind of a Bad Idea

When it Sizzles

Forbidden Billionaires

Take Me, I'm Yours

Make Me Yours

Pretending I'm Yours

The Virgin Playbook

Scored

Screwed

Seduced

Sparked

Scooped

Hot Royal Romance

The Playboy Prince

The Grumpy Prince

The Bossy Prince

Laugh-out-Loud Rocker Rom Coms

The Bangover

Bang Theory

Banging The Enemy

The Rock Star's Baby Bargain

The Bliss River Small Town Series

Falling for the Fling

Falling for the Ex

Falling for the Bad Boy

The Hunter Brothers

The Baby Maker

The Troublemaker

The Heartbreaker

The Panty Melter

Bad Motherpuckers Series

Hot as Puck

Sexy Motherpucker

Puck-Aholic

Puck me Baby

Pucked Up Love

Puck Buddies

Big O Dating Specialists
Romantic Comedies

Hot Revenge for Hire

Hot Knight for Hire

Hot Mess for Hire

Hot Ghosthunter for Hire

The Lonesome Point Series

(Sexy Cowboys)

Leather and Lace

Saddles and Sin

Diamonds and Dust

12 Dates of Christmas

Glitter and Grit

Sunny with a Chance of True Love

Chaps and Chance

Ropes and Revenge

8 Second Angel

The Good Love Series

(co-written with Lauren Blakely)

The V Card

Good with His Hands

Good to be Bad

Made in United States
Orlando, FL
23 December 2024

56456380R00173